'I'd better feed you, then.'

'I don't. . .need to go home,' Laura managed.

'To eggs on toast? You can save them for breakfast. Now are you coming or will I pick you up and carry you?' he demanded.

'You've a gammy leg,' Laura reminded him.

'So I have,' Ben agreed calmly. 'And I agree that it might not take the strain. All it means is that you might get dropped on your very neat bottom between here and the car.'

Dear Reader,

Caroline Anderson's PERFECT HERO has a shock in store, while Dr Laura Haley is determined to pull Dr Ben Durell out of his refuge in Marion Lennox's THE HEALING HEART. We welcome back Sonia Deane, who tackles the thorny question of doctor/patient integrity, while TOMORROW IS ANOTHER DAY by Hazel Fisher explores the recovery of two people who have been badly hurt in the past. Enjoy!

The Editor

Marion Lennox has had a variety of careers—medical receptionist, computer programmer and teacher. Married, with two young children, she now lives in rural Victoria, Australia. Her wish for an occupation which would allow her to remain at home with her children, her dog and the budgie led her to attempt writing a novel.

Recent titles by the same author:

WINGS OF HEALING
A BITTER JUDGEMENT

THE HEALING HEART

BY

MARION LENNOX

MILLS & BOON LIMITED
ETON HOUSE   18–24 PARADISE ROAD
RICHMOND   SURREY   TW9 1SR

First published in Great Britain 1992
by Mills & Boon Limited

© Marion Lennox 1992

Australian copyright 1992
Philippine copyright 1992
This edition 1992

ISBN 0 263 77884 3

Set in 10 on 12 pt Linotron Times
03-9210-52933

Typeset in Great Britain by Centracet, Cambridge
Made and printed in Great Britain

CHAPTER ONE

DR LAURA HALEY'S crowning glory was her red hair, but until now she wouldn't have said she had a temper to match. There had been few times in her twenty-six years where she had been in danger of losing it completely. This, though, was one of them.

'I'm sorry, Dr Haley, but Dr Durell won't see you.' Matron Palmer's voice was implacable. 'I know his views, however, and I know he agrees with me. Sunset Lodge is an efficiently run retirement home, and we've no intention of permitting an over-zealous, inexperienced young doctor to interfere with its operation.'

Laura took a deep breath and struggled to stay calm. 'If Dr Durell owns this place then I need to see him,' she said quietly.

'Dr Durell has better things to do than waste his time on foolishness. If you have any complaints they will be passed on by me.'

If she had any complaints. . . Count to ten, Laura told herself. You're not going to do anyone any good by losing your temper.

'When Mrs Wade came to see me I assumed she was mistaken,' she said out loud. 'She and her husband are both in their eighties and very frail. I advised them to consider entering Sunset Lodge.'

'And we're prepared to take them.' Matron Palmer smiled, as though she didn't see what the fuss was about.

'But she tells me you're putting them in separate

parts of the building!' Laura burst out. 'Dora and Charlie Wade have been married for fifty-seven years, and you insist on separating them!'

Matron's fixed smile didn't slip. 'It's easier for my staff to have women in one wing and men in another,' she said firmly. 'It saves all sorts of nonsense.'

'Oh, for heaven's sake!' Laura put her hands on her slim hips and stared incredulously at the businesslike older woman. 'What nonsense are you suggesting Dora and Charlie could get up to?'

'Don't be coarse.' The matron stood up and walked over to the door. 'Is that all you wanted, Dr Haley? I have work to do.'

'No, it's not.' Laura stood her ground. She had come to see for herself just what sort of place Sunset Lodge was, and had been horrified. A junior nurse had cheerfully shown Calua Bay's new general practitioner around and answered her questions, oblivious to Laura's shocked reaction.

'This place is dreadful!' Laura went on, her clear green eyes flashing anger. A voice at the back of her head was urging caution, but the matron's contemptuous dismissal was too much. 'It's the only retirement home in town, it costs a fortune to get in, and it's worse than any home I've ever been in.'

'Are you accusing us of negligence?' The matron's voice was as cold as ice.

'Oh, no.' Laura shook her head decisively. 'You—or Dr Durell if he owns the place—are far too clever for that. The residents are scrupulously clean and tidy. Any resident who can't dress him or herself is kept in bed, and the others are lined up like zombies in front of the television.' Laura paused for a moment, thinking back to the ward she had just visited.

'They were watching children's television when I walked in this morning,' she said angrily. 'Mature members of this community—all expected to be satisfied with *Toy Time*. For those who didn't want to watch, there was no alternative—and as far as I could see there was no alternative for the rest of the day.' She shrugged. 'I've seen old people physically neglected with more cheer in the ward than these have.'

'There's nothing wrong with the way we run this home,' Matron snapped. 'We keep within health-department guide-lines.'

'I'll bet you do,' Laura agreed. 'To the letter of the law. With the fees you charge you'll be making a fortune.' Laura pushed back her brilliant auburn curls, frustrated with herself as well as with the woman before her. She had only been in the town for just over a week. Her employment wasn't definite and until it was she knew she shouldn't interfere. She couldn't help herself, though. These weary old people seemed to have no one else to fight their cause.

'I want to see the owner,' she said again. 'I want to see Dr Durell.'

'I told you,' Matron said coldly. 'Dr Durell is not available.'

'Why not? Doesn't he live here?'

The matron shook her head. 'He lives here. But he doesn't see visitors.'

'He'll see me,' Laura said grimly.

'Kylie, what do you know about Dr Ben Durell?'

It was the end of the afternoon clinic. Laura had farewelled her last patient and was watching her receptionist file the last cards for the day.

Kylie looked up and flashed a freckle-faced grin. At seventeen, she wasn't the most efficient receptionist Laura had ever worked with, but her cheerful good humour made up for a lot.

'He's the phantom of Calua Bay,' she said mysteriously.

'Come off it, Kylie.' Laura was tired and hungry, and there were still three house calls to do before she was free to stop work.

Kylie's smile deepened and she bent again over the cards. 'That's all I know,' she said. 'When he first came to the town everyone talked about him, but hardly anyone's met him. Mum says there was a tragedy years ago. His wife was killed and he was injured.' Kylie's voice sank to an impressive, theatrical whisper. 'He bought a property up on Blackwood Ridge and sits there, mourning for his love.'

Laura smiled at Kylie's hushed whisper. 'And how long has he been "mourning for his love"?'

'Oh, years and years,' Kylie said airily. 'For as long as I can remember. He must be quite old now. Local rumour has it that he writes, but I don't know what. Probably murder mysteries.'

'Why murder mysteries?'

'That's what recluses do,' Kylie said knowledgeably. 'Or ghastly poetry. I should think it must be mysteries, though, because there's not a lot of money in poetry.'

'So he's rich?'

'Fabulously.' Kylie frowned. 'At least, that's what the locals think. When Sunset Lodge was going to close a few years ago he bought it, just like that. Perhaps he thought he might need it one day,' she said thoughtfully.

'So how can I find this mystery man?' Laura probed.

Matron had refused point-blank to give her an address. 'Does he ever come into town?'

'Oh, no,' Kylie breathed. 'No one sees him. He's got a man working for him who collects his mail and groceries, and Joe won't tell anyone anything.' Kylie's voice contained frustration. 'He says it's more than his job's worth to talk.' Her tone sank again. 'I believe he's horribly scarred.'

Laura sighed. 'So I'm going to have to go out to Blackwood Ridge.' It was five miles out of town, and where she was going to fit it into an already crowded week she didn't know.

'Oh, he won't see you,' Kylie said airily. 'He won't see anyone.'

Laura thought back to the grim group of old people, lined up in front of the television that morning. They were waiting for death in regimented neatness.

'He'll see me,' she repeated for the second time that day.

Three days later Laura had done nothing about seeing the 'phantom'. Whenever she lifted her head there was more work facing her, and she was starting to wonder how the last doctor had coped alone.

'He doesn't get as much work,' Kylie said when asked. 'Dr Paige doesn't encourage patients. He's not nice to people the way you are, Dr Haley. People go to one of the bigger towns rather than put up with him.'

Laura frowned. She didn't know Cliff Paige very well, having responded to the job as locum via an advertisement in a medical journal. He had been practising in Calua Bay for five years, but it seemed he had never had his heart in it. He had certainly done

nothing to interfere with the regimented running of
Sunset Lodge.

'For instance,' Kylie kept on. She motioned to the
retreating back of the last patient. 'You've seen Mrs
Cossels twice this week. I didn't have to remind you of
her name on the second visit, and I heard you asking
about her husband. Dr Paige has been seeing her for
five years and I still have to put her card in front of
him before he remembers who she is. And he never
asks questions about families. He reckons it causes
complications—makes patients stop and chat when he
could be seeing the next one. If you go on like this, the
practice will be run off its feet before Dr Paige comes
back.'

If he comes back, Laura thought to herself. Cliff
Paige was in the city, taking his examinations for
surgery. He'd failed them five years ago, before he had
come here. If he failed them again he'd be back, and
Laura would again be out of a job. She was 'locum
with view'. If he didn't return and she liked the job,
Calua Bay could be Laura's new home.

'Well, I just have to practise my way,' she shrugged
to Kylie. 'I can't be rude to people just to lighten my
work-load.'

'Oh, I don't mind,' the young receptionist reassured
her. She was enjoying the change in the atmosphere of
the clinic since this slim, big-eyed girl had taken over
the Calua Bay practice, and the whole town was talking
about the new lady doctor. Already there were whispered hopes that she might be permanent, and Kylie
was inclined to hope so too.

'When am I going to get out to Blackwood Ridge,
Kylie?' Laura sighed. She was staring hopelessly at her
day-book. 'There's no time.'

'There's no one booked before ten on Friday,' Kylie said helpfully. 'Why don't you go then?'

Laura frowned. It was either that or go at the weekend, though, and she wanted to make the visit as formal as possible. A weekend visit wasn't really appropriate. She needed to get things changed quickly. The Wades mustn't be separated, and the Wades needed care now. 'OK, don't book me,' she told Kylie.

On Friday morning Laura woke with the dawn. She lay for a couple of moments, savouring the stillness of the early morning before the rush of the day ahead. There was a kookaburra cackling to itself in the gum-tree above her hospital flat, and in the distance the soothing murmur of the sea.

The hospital was high on a hill overlooking the ocean. The township of Calua Bay nestled on the narrow strip of land between the mountains and the sea, on the southern coast of New South Wales. The buildings of the town were scattered over any available flat land where the Calua river swept down from the highlands to meet the sea.

It was a magic spot. Laura rose and crossed to the window, soaking in the sight of the dawn over the ocean. This place was just what she wanted to drive away the memories of the bleak days behind her. Good country practices were hard to find, though, and this one had the decided disadvantage of maybe only being temporary.

She was hoping desperately that it wasn't. Even now, when it was so much busier than she had expected, she wasn't regretting it. It was hard work, but more and more she was feeling that it was a job she was suited to.

She was going to miss her swim this morning. Usually she rose at this hour and drove her little car down to the beach for half an hour in the surf before the day began. This morning she was going to have to forfeit the luxury in order to front the reclusive Dr Durell.

She dressed with care, trying for a professional appearance. Usually she favoured soft print dresses, which she covered with her white coats, but this morning her white coat was inappropriate. Her dresses made her look too young, she thought dispassionately. Although she was twenty-six, with her diminutive figure and her unruly curls she had trouble looking nearly that age. And this morning she wanted to appear businesslike and professional.

Finally she chose a crisp linen suit in a soft lilac. With short sleeves, it was not too hot. A dress would be cooler, but if she was lucky she would have time to change again when she returned before morning surgery.

After dressing she stayed staring at the big mirror in her room, surveying herself critically. She still looked too young, but there was nothing she could do about that. Her huge green eyes were too large for her elfin face, and she often had trouble convincing others that she was indeed a qualified medical practitioner. She grinned at herself in the mirror. 'You need to change that red hair to grey,' she told herself. 'Then maybe you'll earn yourself some respect.

'And you'd better hold on to your temper this morning,' her reflection told her. 'A bit of quiet dignity is in order if Dr Ben Durell is to give you a hearing.'

Laura did a quick ward-round in the eight-bed hospital before climbing into her car and turning away from the town. She drove slowly out around the coast road towards Blackwood Ridge, wary of the hairpin bends on the roads hewn from the cliff. Below her, the vast Pacific Ocean stretched to eternity.

Three miles out of town she turned off the highway and started the long haul uphill. The scenery around her was spectacular. The forest on the ridge was wild and free. There were deep gullies filled with ferns of every description, many of them towering above her car. As she emerged into the sun the gums started their skyward journey, each vying with its neighbour for the light. The road was a narrow tree-lined tunnel, with the weak morning sun filtering through from the east.

Laura slowed even further, soaking in the scenery. Gradually, though, she was becoming concerned. She looked down at the rough map Kylie had drawn her and frowned. Surely there could be no farm up here? The land was wilderness. Then she rounded a hairpin bend and braked sharply. Had she seen a gate?

She reversed the car carefully. A rough, winding track led off through the trees. Fifty feet from the road, shrouded by undergrowth and a twist in the track, was a five-bar gate.

There was no sign; no indication of what lay beyond. Laura checked Kylie's map again. There was nothing else up here. This had to be it.

Rather to her surprise, the gate was unlocked. Laura swung it open, drove through and then stopped again to close it. She might be a city doctor but she had learned the rules of the bush fast. Whatever was closed had to be left closed.

It was still early, only a little past eight. The rough bush track meandered through dense forest, climbing upward. Laura opened the window of her car, enjoying the smells and sounds of the bush.

Where on earth was she landing herself? There was no house in view, just a seemingly endless track to nowhere. She was committed now, though. There was no place here to turn the car, and to reverse the way she had come was beyond her skill.

What sort of a man was this Ben Durell? Surely this wasn't a suitable place for an elderly invalid to live? There seemed to be no flat land, and no clearing. Then the car nosed its way around a bend in the track, and Laura gasped in amazement.

The house looked as if it had been carved into the hill. It was all of natural timber, set back where the hill swept inward in a natural hollow. There were vast wooden beams supporting the house, and winding stairs leading up to the enclosed building.

A mass of bougainvillaea twisted around the beams and along the railings of the balcony. Towering eucalpyts dwarfed the house and shrouded it with an air of protection and belonging. Above the rock face at the side of the house a natural waterfall cascaded crystal-clear water into a dammed rocky pool. It made a swimming hole that begged to be used. Two vast loungers in muted green canvas lay invitingly beside the clear water.

Laura gazed upward, open-mouthed. She had never seen such an idyllic setting. As she looked, the big french windows opened from the house. A man walked out on to the balcony and looked down.

'What do you want?' He was short, balding and grumpy. Laura took a deep breath.

'Dr Durell?'

'No.' His voice was as welcoming as a douche of cold water.

'Is this his place?'

'That's none of your business. You're trespassing, lady.'

Laura's lips tightened. She felt a fool, standing beneath the balcony, yelling up at the unwelcoming man above, but she didn't intend to have come all this way for nothing.

'I want to speak to Dr Durell, please.'

'Dr Durell doesn't see visitors, especially. . .' he drew out the word '. . . those he doesn't know. Now would you like to turn your car around and get out of here?'

'No, I would not.' To her dismay, Laura felt her temper taking hold yet again. 'I need to speak to Dr Durell.'

'Anything you need to say can be said by letter. Dr Durell has a post-box in town.'

'What I need to say will be said in person,' Laura said savagely.

'That's not possible.'

'Well, you can give a message to Dr Durell from me,' Laura said. She flicked her red hair back and let loose her anger. 'You can tell him the next edition of the *South Coast Times* is going to have a front-page story detailing just how much money his nursing home makes from its unfortunate inhabitants. It's going to detail the ghastly lifestyle of the residents, and it's going to spell out what the elderly of this town are paying to line the pockets of an uncaring absentee landlord who should be drummed out of the district.' She paused for breath, shocked by the vehemence of the words she had just uttered.

Her outburst was futile. The words had made no impression at all on the man on the balcony.

'I'll tell him.' His voice was blank and non-committal. 'Now leave.'

Laura glared upwards. The man's face was implacable. There was nothing else she could do. She felt colour surge in her cheeks as her frustration rose.

Would she be courageous enough to go to the newspapers? She had little choice now but to do just that. Her reception had only made her angrier than she had already been. She had made a threat and she would carry it through.

'I'm going,' she muttered through clenched teeth. 'Just don't say I didn't warn you.'

'How very melodramatic.'

Laura jumped and swung around. Behind her, on the track beside her car, stood Dr Ben Durell.

She knew at once who he was, although her preconceptions had to change. This man was no elderly invalid. He was in his mid-thirties, she thought; no more.

His injuries told her who he was. His dark tanned face was marred by a disfiguring burn that ran from his brow down the full length of one cheek. It twisted and contorted his eyebrow, making his dark features seem sinister and threatening. By his side he held a stick, which he held as if he needed its support.

He must have been incredibly good-looking before his accident, Laura thought fleetingly, with his dark, aquiline features and tall, muscular body. He still was. In his jeans and casual shirt, he fitted into this place as if he'd been there all his life.

'Dr Durell?' Her voice had lost the harsh note of anger. The anger had been supplanted by shock.

'Yes.' His deep-set eyes were watchful; appraising. 'Who the hell are you?'

'I'm Laura Haley.' She took a breath and fought for composure. 'Dr Laura Haley.' She held out a hand in greeting. 'I'm Calua Bay's general practitioner.'

Ben Durell ignored the outstretched hand. He stood ten feet from her, his eyes cold and unwelcoming.

'Shall I get rid of her for you, Ben?' It was the man above them on the balcony. Ben Durell looked up and shook his head.

'Thanks, Joe,' he said calmly. 'I think I can manage to dispose of this one.' Laura's colour deepened as Joe shrugged and turned inside.

'Now,' Ben Durell said coldly, 'suppose you tell me what that hysterical little performance was all about?'

Laura stood her ground. This man was an arrogant toad, but she had to talk to him.

'It wasn't a hysterical outburst,' she said icily.

'Suppose we let me be the judge of that.'

Anger was again building up in Laura to the point where she felt she would explode. Frantically she fought for control of her temper.

'As you judge what's good for the inmates of Sunset Lodge?' she threw at him.

'Sunset Lodge has nothing to do with me.'

'Do you deny that you own it?'

'Of course I don't.' His voice was weary and uninterested. 'I bought it to stop it being closed. And after my no doubt misplaced philanthropy I left it in the charge of the board who had run it for years.'

Laura nodded. 'And just collected the profits as they appeared in the mail,' she snapped.

Ben Durell's eyes narrowed. He took a step towards her and then stopped.

'Look, I don't know who the hell you are to come prying into something that doesn't concern you,' he said quietly, 'but if I were you I'd go away and do my homework before I started throwing accusations about. Do you have any idea what it costs to run a home like Sunset Lodge?'

'I've a fair idea,' Laura said. 'I've been involved in other homes besides this one. . .' Her voice faltered momentarily but she forced herself on. 'I know what the best ones and worst ones charge and provide. Sunset Lodge takes one section of each. It charges top rates for bottom service.'

'Bottom service. . .' His eyes narrowed and the twisted eyebrow contorted. 'Give me an example.'

'Such as not getting patients up and dressed,' she snapped. 'Such as having three meals within eight hours so you only have to pay for one cooking shift. Such as no occupational therapy. . .'

Ben Durell shrugged. 'Well, Dr Haley or whoever you are, I question your sources of information. I pay for two cooking shifts and a full-time occupational therapist.'

Laura rocked back on her heels. Ben's angry black eyes met her green ones and Laura's defiant stand wavered. Was she wrong?

And then she remembered the rigid lines of chairs and the old, dead eyes turned endlessly to the television screen. Those people weren't filling in time before something happened. Those people had given up hope that anything would ever happen again.

'Either you're a liar or a fool,' she told Ben Durell. Her voice lowered to a whisper. 'There's no occupational therapist in that place. Nothing happens there. Nothing! But you've been ripping off the residents for too long, Dr Durell. You live in luxury while they rot. Well, Sunset Lodge is going to get more exposure in the next week than it's ever had in its life before. And, hermit or not, you're going to be exposed with it.'

Ben Durell took a step towards her, and then another. As the weight went on to his bad leg he limped perceptibly and Laura saw that the knee was stiff and useless. When she looked up he had taken another step and was towering over her.

'You put anything about me in the newspapers and you'll wonder what hit you,' he said menacingly. 'I never asked to get involved when I bought that damned nursing home. I did it because the locals were desperate. If I hadn't bought it the place would have closed and been turned into a holiday resort.'

'And now it's supporting your reclusive habits nicely,' Laura spat at him. Her breath was coming in short gasps. He was too close for comfort.

His face closed in anger as he drew in breath. For one long moment Laura thought he would hit her. She drew back, casting a nervous glance at the house. At least Kylie knew where she had gone.

'Don't worry.' Ben Durell's voice was harsh and mocking. 'I make it a point not to strike women. Even if they are as rude and ignorant as you, Dr Haley.'

'I may be rude, but I'm not a thief, and that's all you are.' Laura was close to tears and her control had crumpled. 'You're ripping the life savings off those people and leaving them with nothing. Nothing!' she choked. 'They stare at a television for day after day and you haven't even the decency to give them colour. Well, I don't care about your insinuating threats, Mr Durell. If you don't give a damn, at least I do.' She turned and stepped back towards the car, flinging open the door. 'I'm going to the newspapers. Right now.'

She pulled shut the door of the car and turned the

key. She still had to turn the car, and the space available was limited by Ben Durell's large body standing in the middle of the turning circle. She'd like to run him down, she thought bitterly. She had never felt so humiliated.

She revved forward and then backward, straining at the wheel. As she reached the limit of the driveway and stopped to change gear her door was flung open and the key removed from the ignition. Ben Durell was staring down at her, a strange look on his face.

'There's a colour television in each patient's room,' he said. 'And my last statement from the board listed the purchase of a large colour screen with stereo sound for both lounges.'

Laura grabbed for the keys and retrieved them from his grasp. 'I don't care what any statement says,' she said harshly. 'The statements can say anything they like, but the patients are watching one black and white television.' She shoved the key in the ignition, turned it and started the car forward. It lurched down the drive in the wrong gear but she was away. What had to be said had been said, and Ben Durell could like it or lump it.

CHAPTER TWO

BY THE time Laura re-entered the hospital grounds she had stopped shaking, but her mind was still in turmoil. Ben Durell had rattled her composure as it hadn't been rattled for a long time.

'Was I unfair to him?' she asked herself. To brand someone a fool or a liar was no light accusation.

'It was because he accused me first,' she said firmly. 'Hysterical. . .rude. . .ignorant. . .' Had she been those things?

Not hysterical. She hadn't been hysterical. Well. . . Not completely. But perhaps she had been rude. And it was true that she didn't understand the running of Sunset Lodge.

Still, Ben Durell was the owner and as the owner the ultimate responsibility was his. He was making the profits and he had to answer to the community as to how those profits were made. And Laura mightn't understand the structure of authority of Sunset Lodge, but she did know that the place was appalling.

'He's not going to like it,' Laura said grimly to the steering-wheel in front of her. 'But he's going to have to come out of hibernation and defend himself.'

And why was he in 'hibernation'? Why was he a recluse? Laura thought back to his injuries. The burn on his face had been repaired by plastic surgery. The skin on one cheek was smoother than the other, and faint scarring lined the burn's surface. Still, the skin grafts had been skilfully done. No one could call Ben

Durell handsome, but his appearance had been strengthened by the scars. The twist to his eyebrow gave a harsh, unrelenting appearance to the stern features.

His leg too was not something he could be embarrassed about in public. The limp was there, but it was not repugnant.

In fact, Laura thought wryly, he's damned attractive. Too attractive. She found herself staring down at the windscreen of the stationary car with the memory of deep, dark eyes and an angry mouth superimposed on the glass. Ben's black hair had been swept back and badly needed a cut. It curled in an unruly mass.

I wonder what it would feel like to touch? she thought.

Laura caught herself with shock as she realised where her thoughts were leading her. Good grief! The last thing Dr Laura Haley wanted was to find a man attractive—any man. And especially not a man she had just finished calling a liar and a fool. She took a firm grip on herself and climbed out of the car.

It was after ten and the clinic was already filling. Kylie greeted her with restrained curiosity in front of the patients, but Laura knew once they were alone she would be barraged by questions. She ignored the girl's raised eyebrows, took the first patient's card and retired to the privacy of her surgery.

From there on her work took over. It was the height of summer and Laura was swamped with tourists as well as the regular townfolk. The tourists presented her with everything from sunburn to heart attacks.

'I'm going to write a paper one day on the relationship between ill health and holidays,' Laura said wearily as Kylie brought in the tenth tourist's card for the morning. 'Why is it that people wait to go on holiday before they fall ill?'

'Perhaps it's because they're feeling down in the dumps anyway and think a holiday might fix them,' Kylie said sagely. 'Anyway, I like the tourists coming in.'

Laura looked out into the reception area and caught sight of a couple of the occupants. A huge, bronzed male who had the build of a surf life-saver was sitting nursing an injured hand. His friend, sitting beside him, was just as good-looking. Laura smiled at Kylie and nodded.

'I see what you mean.'

Kylie blushed and retreated.

There was no time for Laura to have lunch. Her late start had cost her any free time for the day.

I don't know when I'm going to get time to ring the newspaper, she thought ruefully. After threatening Ben Durell she had to make good that threat, but there wasn't time, and she could hardly ask Kylie to contact the newspaper for her. She put it to the back of her mind while she concentrated on the problem at hand; in this instance, Mr Robilliard's piles.

Halfway through her examination the phone rang. She ignored it. There were some things that couldn't be left halfway through, and Mr Robilliard was crimson with embarrassed mortification as it was. Finally Laura finished, bade her relieved patient goodbye and crossed to the phone as it rang again.

'It's Dr Durell.' Kylie's voice was breathless with interest. 'He's been waiting for ages and he sounds cross.'

Still? Laura thought wearily. She sighed. 'OK, Kylie. Put him through.'

'Dr Haley?'

'Yes.' Laura's voice was cautious.

'Good of you to finally answer.'

Laura said nothing. Her mouth tightened to an angry line. If Ben Durell didn't understand the demands of a sole GP practice she didn't have time to enlighten him.

'I need to talk to you.' His voice was as angry as she felt.

'You are talking to me.'

'I mean face to face. Can you be at Sunset Lodge at four this afternoon?'

Laura glanced at her watch and then out to the packed waiting-room. 'No.'

'Why not?'

'Because I'm busy,' she snapped. Laura's stomach was complaining about her missed lunch. She was five patients behind already and was booked solid until six-thirty that night. 'Now, is there anything else? I've a patient waiting.'

There was silence from the other end of the phone. Laura was tempted to replace the receiver on its cradle but wasn't quite game. Finally he spoke again.

'If I tell you I'm personally investigating the running of Sunset Lodge, will you leave contacting the Press for a few days?'

'Why should I?' Laura was being more brusque than she intended, but the man had her tense and nervous.

'Because I asked you to,' Ben Durell was saying.

'Now, there's a good reason,' she flung back sarcastically. 'You'll have to do better than that, Dr Durell.'

'Give me until Monday before you contact them.' It was still a demand.

'What on earth will change before Monday? Are you going to miraculously find fifty television sets?'

'I just might at that, Dr Haley,' he said grimly. 'I just might at that.'

Laura took a deep breath. She didn't have time to talk to the newspaper until Monday anyway, so she might as well admit it. And if he really was going to do something. . .

'All right,' she said ungraciously. 'But if my car gets bombed or my cocoa gets laced with arsenic over the weekend there'll be a letter with my lawyer.'

There was another silence, and, when Ben Durell spoke again, for the first time Laura heard a hint of laughter.

'You underestimate me, Dr Haley. I'd stoop to nothing so crude.'

It was after seven when Laura finished her afternoon surgery. By the time she did, Kylie had already left.

'You don't mind if I go?' she'd whispered as she'd handed Laura the last patient's card. 'I've got a date.'

Laura raised her eyebrows and Kylie blushed. Laura smiled at the girl as she asked a question she couldn't resist.

'The life-saver?'

'He's not really a life-saver,' Kylie whispered, her blush deepening. 'He just looks like one. He's a first-year law student from Sydney.'

'Fast work!' Laura grinned. Then she took pity on the girl and laughed. 'Go on. Hop it. I can manage here. And Kylie?' This as Kylie grabbed her bag and started for the door.

'Yes?'

'Enjoy yourself.'

Laura was still smiling as she ushered in the last patient for the day, a burly farmer with a dislocated thumb. She'd give a lot to be as heart-whole and fancy-free as Kylie again, she thought, and sent up a silent prayer that Kylie would remain so.

Don't let her muck it up, she thought, like me. . .

Mr Creighton's thumb was quick to reduce, but he was a talker. He was intensely interested in the new lady doctor and assumed Laura was as interested in him as he was in her. Laura had to admit that she enjoyed his talk and, with no more patients waiting, openly encouraged him. Her stark little hospital flat was not appealing. After a fortnight in the town she was finding the going lonely.

Finally she showed the farmer out of the surgery, and as she did so another car turned into the car park. She gave an inward groan. It was all very well wanting company but she needed to eat. She'd had an apple and three cups of coffee since breakfast. Then as she stood waiting at the door her heart gave a sickening lurch. She recognised the long, lean figure unwinding himself from the seat of the Range Rover. It was Ben Durell.

For a moment all she wanted to do was walk into the building, slam the door and lock it. It was too late, of course. He had seen her. Retrieving his stick from the car, he limped towards her.

'Dr Haley.' His tone was cautious, and Laura answered in kind.

'Dr Durell.'

'I hoped I might catch you here.'

She said nothing.

'I want you to come with me to Sunset Lodge.' His

voice was firm and sure, that of a man used to getting his own way.

'Now?' Laura said, stunned.

'Yes.' He looked over her shoulder into the empty reception area. 'I take it you've finished for the day.'

'My work, yes,' Laura said icily. 'I do have other things to do.'

He nodded. 'Your social life, of course,' he said silkily. 'How foolish of me. It is Friday night, after all.'

'If you can call social life going home and making myself eggs on toast then yes, it's my social life,' Laura said, between gritted teeth. 'But I've had one apple since breakfast, breakfast was toast at five-thirty this morning, and I'm starving. I've no intention of letting you or your blasted nursing home stand in the way of me and food. Now if you'll excuse me.' She turned back into the room and started putting away Mr Creighton's card. When she looked up again Ben was still there, leaning on the open door and watching her.

'You don't need to diet.' His eyes were on the curves of her slim figure, raking her from head to toe. His look was all at once complimentary and intensely personal. Laura flushed.

'I am not dieting!' Her words echoed loudly round the empty room and she flushed. Lowering her tone deliberately, she continued, 'I don't know what sort of doctor you are, Ben Durell, but you've either never been in country general practice or you've been out of touch a long time. I'm the only doctor in this place at the height of the tourist season. I'm run off my feet. I had four hours' sleep last night. I was up at five-thirty so that I could wedge in a visit to you, waste of time as it was, and I haven't had a break all day.' She glared at him, her voice rising to a high-pitched squeak.

'You firstly demand I take time off in the middle of
a frantic afternoon, and now you stand there treating
me like some idle little socialite whom you can just
beckon with the crook of a little finger. . . Well, you
can just shove it, Ben Durell. Get lost!'

To her horror, Laura felt tears welling at the back of
her eyes. The combination of two weeks of over-work,
not enough sleep, the arguments of the day and nothing
to eat became too much. With a gasp she turned away,
fumbling in the pocket of her white coat for a
handkerchief.

Even more to her horror, he didn't leave. Through
her distress she heard his footsteps behind her, the
heavy sound of his cane, and then a large linen
handkerchief was placed firmly into her free hand. His
voice, when he finally spoke, had changed. It sounded
tense and suddenly tired.

'I think I might be forced to apologise.'

'Don't strain yourself,' Laura said waspishly as she
found her voice again. She blew her nose hard, looked
down at Ben's handkerchief and finally gave a watery
giggle. 'Thanks for the loan. Can I give it back now?'

'Consider it a gift,' Ben said promptly. 'A peace
offering. Now. . .' He looked down at the redheaded
girl standing before him, his scarred eyebrow crooked
in thought. He didn't have a clue what to make of this
woman. She oscillated between being a shrill-voiced
shrew and a child. And something else, he conceded.
Her flaming hair wisped and curled in a mass to her
shoulders. Her tear-drenched green eyes were huge in
her face. . .

'I suppose I'd better feed you, then,' he said.

'I don't. . . I need to go home,' Laura managed.

'To eggs on toast? You can save them for breakfast.

Now are you coming or will I pick you up and carry you?' he demanded.

'You've a gammy leg,' Laura reminded him.

'So I have,' he agreed calmly. 'And I agree that it might not take the strain. But it wouldn't stop me from giving it my best shot. All it means is that you might get dropped on your very neat bottom somewhere between here and the car.'

Laura flashed a glance up at him. His eyes were smiling but his look was implacable. . .relentless. This man knew what he wanted, and knew how to get it. She shank back instinctively.

'N. . .no.'

'Yes,' he said, just as quietly. 'I need to talk to you and you need food. Now are you going to come or am I going to have to drag you?'

Laura cast another glance at him and conceded. There seemed no way out.

They drove in silence down into Calua Bay. In the main street were a couple of brightly lit restaurants, but Ben didn't slow down. He drove until he reached the foreshore. On the beach-side drive was an open-air café. Ben pulled the car into the car park.

'Wait there,' he said curtly.

'Yes, sir,' Laura muttered under her breath.

She watched him limp over to the stalls and make his purchases. Here the lighting was dim. She could see people make way for the man with his cane and see them cast curious glances at him as they moved aside. Was this why he hadn't taken her to a restaurant? Was he self-conscious about his appearance?

Finally he returned, his free hand carrying a variety of plastic bags.

'Dinner, ma'am,' he said gravely. 'In the car or on the beach?'

Not at one of the tables under the lights, Laura noted. She frowned. Surely such an arrogant male couldn't be afraid of being seen?

'On the beach, please,' she said quietly. It was a glorious, wind-free summer evening and the surf and sand were calling her. She was regretting badly her missed swim of the morning.

Ben retrieved a rug from the truck. They made their way down across the still warm, loose sand near the rocks, and on to the firmer sand of last night's high tide. Here they could eat without spoiling their food with sand. Ben spread the rug and emptied his bags.

To Laura's hungry gaze the food was magnificent. There were slivers of whiting done in crunchy golden batter, calamari rings with fresh wedges of lemon, and piles and piles of crisp French fries. There was a container of lettuce and tiny cherry tomatoes, a bowl of huge red strawberries with masses of thick cream and, as the *pièce de résistance*, an opened bottle of ice-cold white wine.

'It's only paper cups, though,' Ben apologised.

'I can stand it,' Laura reassured him. She looked down at the fragrant food before her. 'Can I start?'

'Be my guest.'

Twenty minutes later she finally came to a halt. She ate her last strawberry, ran a finger inelegantly around the container and licked it with regret. She looked up to find Ben Durell watching her with amusement.

'I take back what I said about the diet,' he grinned. 'I've never seen a woman eat so much.'

'You've never seen a woman as hungry as I was,' she told him. 'Thank you.'

'My pleasure.'

She continued to watch him, her brows creased in puzzlement. 'Do you often come down here?'

'When I can't stand Joe's or my cooking. The food is far better here than in the restaurants in the main street.'

'How do you know?'

'I remember,' he said before he could stop himself. There was a long silence.

'You mean you haven't been in them since after your accident?' Laura probed gently.

'No.' He stood up quickly, stumbling as he put his weight on to his bad leg. Laura handed him his cane. She stayed where she was, sitting on the rug at his feet. 'Are you ready to go?' he demanded.

Laura rose then, but shook her head. 'I'm sorry,' she said. 'But you can't bring me to the beach and not let me feel the sea. I'll be back in a moment.'

She pulled off her sandals and threw them on to the rug, dug her toes into the warm sand and headed for the waves.

She had changed after she came back from her visit to Blackwood Ridge that morning into one of her favoured big floral-print dresses. It was caught with a wide belt at the waist and billowed into a huge skirt. Laura lifted her skirt with both hands and ran lightly into the foam.

The water was delicious on her hot feet and tired mind. Ignoring the man waiting on the beach, she turned deliberately away and started walking, kicking up a spray of salt water as she went. The waves ran in and in again, catching the hem of her skirt. She could feel the spray on her face, and it dissolved the troubles of her day.

Always the sea did this to her. This was why she had taken the position in Calua Bay. Despite the overwork, despite the problems of Sunset Lodge, despite Dr Ben Durell, if she could have this—the sea and the sand between her toes—she would be content.

She turned and looked up at the man waiting above her on the beach.

'Come on in,' she called. 'It's lovely.'

He didn't respond. The great Ben Durell wouldn't stoop to taking his shoes off, rolling up his trousers and risking a wetting, Laura thought maliciously. A wave larger than most came surging around her, soaking the hem of her dress. Laura looked down, an imp of mischief welling within her, then suddenly bent, scooped handfuls of the lovely cool sea and directed it straight at the man on the sand.

It didn't quite reach. She saw the bulk of the water spray on to the dry sand at his feet, and by the time it did she was already regretting her crazy impulse. Ben Durell wasn't a man you threw water at.

In the dim light she saw him look down at the cane at his side, and she knew suddenly that he was torn. One part of him wanted to throw the thing away and join the breathless girl in the surf.

The aloof and humourless recluse won the day. He stood motionless. 'When you're quite ready, Dr Haley,' he said coldly.

Laura bit her lip. She was being stupid. For one crazy instant she had tried to treat him as a human being and a friend. She looked at his dark figure on the beach. Ben Durell was no longer that. He had cut himself off from human contact years ago.

Finally she walked up the beach with regret. Ben Durell was waiting. Sunset Lodge was waiting. Her time of not being Dr Laura Haley, general practitioner, was over.

Ben didn't speak when she reached him. He had folded the rug, disposed of the remnants of their meal and was waiting. Laura cast a cautious glance up at him, hit as she did so with a wave of compunction. Had it been mean of her to taunt him like that?

He could have joined her, she reminded herself. His leg didn't seem so bad that he couldn't remove his shoes and roll up his trousers. But then, supercilious males didn't paddle, Laura decided, and Ben Durell was one supercilious male.

'Are you still taking me to Sunset Lodge?' Laura asked as they climbed into the truck again.

'Yes,' he told her. 'That's the price of the meal.' He glanced across at her and smiled. 'That is, if you can make a tour of inspection with sand between your toes.'

'I can do anything with sand between my toes,' Laura said with dignity.

There was silence as they drove. Pulling into the home's car park, Laura frowned.

'You realise you won't be very welcome,' she said.

'I know,' Ben told her. 'In fact, I've never been here. That's why I'm taking you. As you're the town doctor, they can hardly refuse you admission.'

'You've really never been here?' Laura stared at him. 'But you own it!'

He parked the truck and swung round to face her. 'Look, let's get one fact straight, Dr Haley: I bought this place because it was being closed. It's an hour's drive to the nearest nursing home and I thought it was lousy that the town was going to lose this facility. If one of an elderly couple has to go into care it's not right that the other is too far away to visit them. But after putting my money into the place, after saving its existence, I bowed out. The place was left in the charge of its former administrators.'

'A board made up of people as elderly as most of the residents,' Laura said softly. She had queried Kylie about it earlier in the day.

'It's headed by a competent accountant,' Ben told her. 'Craig Palmer.'

'Craig Palmer. . .' Laura said the word on a long note of discovery. All of a sudden things were starting to fall into place. 'And the matron is Lucy Palmer.'

'I don't have a clue who the staff are,' Ben said firmly. 'That's left to the board.'

'To Craig Palmer.' Laura let the words hang. She turned and started climbing from the truck. 'OK, let's make this tour, then,' she said quietly. 'But when I told you we wouldn't be very welcome I wasn't talking about you being a stranger. I was talking about the time. It's eight-thirty at night, and lights out for residents is eight.'

In the soft light thrown by the entrance windows Laura saw Ben frown. 'That's nonsense,' he said briskly. 'It's Friday night. Every Friday night there's entertainment with the town's folk trio or visiting artists.'

'According to your statement, I'll bet,' Laura said drily.

Ben's mouth tightened into a grim line. Without another word he turned and strode to the door.

Laura stood back and watched him. His stride was that of an angry man, scenting deception. And when he reached the door she nodded to herself before following. He had left his cane in the truck.

Ben didn't miss it. He limped slightly, but he didn't need his cane as he strode from room to room. The startled junior nurse who had opened the door was pushed aside as Ben made his inspection.

The place was in darkness. Ben ignored the girl's frightened protests. He turned on lights and looked everywhere.

The residents were mostly asleep, and Laura noted that few of them woke as they flicked on lights and walked from room to room. The few who woke seemed dazed and disorientated, drifting off again into sleep almost immediately.

'How the hell do you get them to sleep so early?' Ben demanded of the timid nurse scuttling behind him.

'Please. . . I'll have to get the supervisor,' she pleaded. 'She's over in the other wing.'

'Are you the only staff member in this wing?' Ben demanded. The girl was all of seventeen.

'Y. . .yes. There's Mrs Selleck in the other wing.'

'The supervisor. Is she a trained nurse?'

'N. . .no. I don't think so.'

'Are you?'

'I did six months' nursing training,' the girl said defensively.

'And failed your first exams, I'll bet,' Ben growled. He flicked on the light of another ward. Six bodies lay sleeping in regimented lines. 'Why the hell don't they wake?'

'I can tell you that,' Laura said quietly from behind him. 'When I was here the other day I was reminded that the scripts for sleeping-pills needed renewing.'

Ben turned on her. 'You prescribe them?' he demanded incredulously.

'Of course I don't.' Laura cringed for the town's

former doctor, but Cliff Paige was going to have to defend himself on this one. 'I've only been in the town for a little over two weeks, though. The old scripts are still current.'

'So these patients are drugged.'

'These residents,' Laura corrected him quietly. 'This is a mobile ward. These men are still capable of dressing and showering themselves, and basic self-care. They're not ill. They're mostly just too old to be at home on their own.'

She didn't know whether Ben heard her. His eyes were on a bare wooden stand at the side of the room.

'Is a television meant to go there?' he asked the nurse.

'I. . . I don't know,' she stuttered. She cast a pleading look at Laura for guidance. 'I. . . There's never been one since I started working here.'

'And when was that?'

'Only three months ago,' she admitted. She cast a last imploring glance at Laura. 'Look—I'm going to get the supervisor.'

'Do what you like.' Ben's face was as black as thunder and Laura and the nurse might have just as well not been there. He strode out of the room, flicking the switch off behind him, leaving Laura to negotiate her way to the door in the dark.

When she reached the passage he had gone. Then she saw him emerge from the lounge and stride down towards the office at the front of the building. His limp was becoming less pronounced as he grew angrier. She walked slowly to the door of the office and stood watching as he pulled open drawer after drawer. He upended boxes of computer paper, leaving the paper strewn on the floor, and started heaping files into the boxes.

'What are you doing?' Laura asked mildly.

'I'm being taken for a ride,' he said savagely. 'What does it look like.'

Laura grinned. She was starting to enjoy herself very much. This was Lucy Palmer's office, and Laura had her own small vendetta with Matron Palmer. 'This is for Dora and Charlie Wade,' she promised the absent matron. 'And the rest of the residents of this place.'

The filing cabinet at the side of the desk was locked. Ben wrenched at it and swore savagely. He looked around, his eyes lighting on the metal base of a desk light. It took him moments to pull the light off the base, giving him a straight, heavy metal rod. Moments after that the lock of the filing cabinet was a twisted mess. Ben prised the drawers out, one after another, and more files joined the growing heap in the boxes.

There was a commotion outside; the sound of a siren, a door flung upon, raised female voices and heavy footsteps. Ben kept silently sorting through the files, throwing the ones he wanted into the pile. Laura looked up as a large police officer appeared at the door. Behind him was a middle-aged woman, the supervisor, Laura assumed, and behind her the frightened face of the little nurse.

Laura recognised the sergeant. Dr Paige had taken her down to the police station and introduced her to the small force before he had left. In a town as small as this there were often times when the police and the doctor had to work together.

She smiled at his stunned face and tried to think of something to say. 'Good evening, Sergeant,' she finally

managed in a weak voice. Beside her, Ben didn't even
look up.

'Who the hell is this?' The police officer walked into
the paper-strewn room and stared around in amazement. 'I had a report of a break-in.' He stared across
at Ben and took a step towards him.

'We can hardly have broken in,' Laura said firmly,
placing a restraining hand on his arm. 'I'm the home's
official doctor at the moment, and Dr Durell is the
owner. Dr Durell seems to think the residents here are
being short-changed at his expense,' she said softly.
She hesitated and then continued, 'He feels there may
be some discrepancies in the files.'

'Well, well.' The policeman had stopped short in
amazement. 'So this is our hermit!'

Ben retrieved the last file from the bottom drawer,
stacked the boxes on top of each other and picked
them up. At last he turned to the four watching people.

'I think I have everything I need,' he told Laura
curtly. He nodded to the policeman. 'Is there anything
I can do for you?'

The policeman surveyed him thoughtfully, and then
his face slowly relaxed into a grin.

'Do I take it that the absent owner is finally taking a
hand in the running of this dump?' he smiled.

Ben's face remained expressionless. 'I might be,' he
said.

The police officer stood aside. 'Well, be my guest,'
he said expansively. 'Can I help carry anything out?'

Ben shook his head and made to leave. Then, as he
reached the door, he stopped and faced the uniformed
sergeant.

'Why so helpful?'

'My mother's in this place,' the policeman admitted.

'She has Alzheimer's disease and my dad can't cope. I know how much we pay to keep her in here and I know what happens to her. Nothing! The nursing home up the coast is half the price and the residents get much more. If Dad could bear to have her so far away we'd shift her.' He looked thoughtfully down at the box Ben was carrying. 'If what you're doing means change, then I reckon I'm all for it. This place can't possibly get any worse.'

For the first time Ben's features relaxed and he permitted himself the ghost of a smile. 'This place might just be going to get a whole lot better,' he said softly. He stared sightlessly down at the mess of files. 'If you could, I'd be grateful if you could prevent the Palmers leaving town until I've spent some time with my lawyer.'

He turned and strode down the passage, with Laura almost running to keep up with him.

CHAPTER THREE

LAURA helped Ben load the files into the truck. Behind them she heard the policeman take his leave of the still protesting supervisor.

'There's nothing I can do,' she heard him say. 'Dr Durell owns the place and Dr Haley is medical director. I can hardly stop them reading their own files.'

'But they've broken things.' The supervisor's voice was a wail. 'He's smashed the filing cabinet. . .'

'It's his filing cabinet,' the policeman said firmly, and turned away. Sergeant Robins had done his duty as he saw it.

As the police car nosed out of the car park and away down the road the supervisor came across the car park to Laura.

'I've just phoned the matron,' she threatened. 'She's coming now.'

Laura looked up at Ben and he shrugged.

'I want to go through this stuff before I see her,' he said. 'She can wait.' He held open the passenger door of his truck for Laura. 'Get in,' he ordered. 'I'll run you back to the hospital.'

They didn't speak as they drove the half-mile to the hospital on the hill above the town. Laura's thoughts were racing, but there was nothing she could think of to say. She glanced across at the silent face of the man at her side. His face was grim and the scar of the burn was stretched tightly across his face.

'Would you like to have coffee here before the drive

home?' she asked hesitantly as they pulled up at the entrance to her hospital flat. Laura was still nervous of the man, but to offer him coffee seemed the least she could do. He was going to have to face Lucy Palmer, and if Ben Durell scared Laura then Lucy Palmer made her knees knock. She's a mean piece of work, Laura thought to herself. To drug those old people. . .

'Thank you,' Ben said curtly. He swung himself out of the truck and winced as his weight went on to his bad leg. He reached back for his cane.

'You know, you walked quite well without it back there,' Laura commented.

'You're not catching me out in something I don't know,' Ben said heavily. 'I can walk without it.'

'It just hurts when you do.'

'Yes. Now do you mind leaving off the inquisition.'

'When was the last time you had physiotherapy?'

He stopped and swung around to face her in the dim light. 'Four years ago,' he said harshly. 'Dr Haley, you are not my doctor, so butt out of what is not your business.'

'Who is your doctor?'

She heard the intake of angry breath. Ben Durell, she thought, was doomed to stay angry with her forever.

'I take care of myself. I haven't a medical degree for nothing.'

'So you are a medical doctor,' Laura said slowly. 'Why aren't you practising?'

'Because I don't want to. Now if you're going to make me a cup of coffee then I accept with pleasure. It's been a long day and I've a demanding drive in front of me. But if I'm to face any more questions then I'll leave you now.'

Laura looked up at the dark, grim face of the man at her side and laughed. 'OK, Dr Durell,' she smiled. 'No more questions tonight.'

'No more questions, period,' he said harshly.

'Oh, come on, now.' Laura fumbled in her bag for her key and unlocked the door to her little flat. 'That's hardly fair. I've an insatiable curiosity.'

'Is that what made you interested in Sunset Lodge?' he said sarcastically.

Laura flicked on the lights and they entered the sparsely furnished apartment. It was neat and functional, but nothing else. 'Good grief,' Ben said softly, staring around him. 'Is this where the town houses its only doctor? No wonder they can't get a competent. . .' He stopped, as if he had just realised what he had said.

Laura smiled thinly, choosing to ignore the slight. 'I could have used Cliff Paige's house but it's down on the beach, and I thought it would be easier if I was nearer the hospital,' she said tightly. She crossed to the kitchen. 'And no, it wasn't my insatiable curiosity that led me to investigate Sunset Lodge.' She turned her back on Ben while she made coffee and quietly told him about the Wades.

'You will let them share a room, won't you?' she asked softly as she handed him a mug of the steaming brew. She looked up at him and found his eyes on hers. He was frowning again, but his dark eyes were no longer angry. They were looking at her as if he was seeing something he didn't understand. She tried to meet his look, but her gaze fell away as she felt her colour rising. He was too damned close.

'I. . . What will you do with the papers?' she asked, trying to keep an unaccountable tremor from her voice.

'I'll put them in the lawyer's hands tomorrow,' Ben

said, his frowning gaze still on the girl before him.
'Correlating them with the statements I've been getting
should be a legal wonderland.'

'They won't match.'

Ben took a mouthful of coffee and laughed. 'I should
imagine they read as if they're for two separate nursing
homes,' he said bluntly. 'Believe it or not, Sunset
Lodge has made no profit for years. I was prepared to
put up with it. The running costs were exorbitant but I
didn't want any place I was associated with to provide
poor service. According to my statements, the home
has occupational therapists, entertainment, outings. . .
It's been repainted inside and out. . . I could go on
forever. None of those things fit with what I've seen
tonight or what you've accused me of.'

Laura winced. 'I'm sorry,' she said quietly. 'But
really, if it was your nursing home then you had a
responsibility to check.'

He stared down at her, his face closed. 'Well,' he
said at last, 'I've checked now. Satisfied, Dr Haley?'

Laura shook her head. 'Not until you've fixed it, Dr
Durell,' she said firmly.

'I've no intention of personally "fixing it",' he told
her shortly. 'Perhaps I could pay you a wage as medical
director to oversee the changes that will have to be
made?'

Laura shook her head. 'I can't promise that,' she
told him. 'I don't know yet whether I'm permanent,
and I certainly haven't time to take on any more work.'
She shrugged. 'Though I doubt if Cliff Paige will take
on the role if he returns.'

'Not if he's written those prescriptions,' Ben said, his
voice suddenly savage. 'Damn the man. I could have
him struck off for that.'

Laura looked curiously up at him. 'I could have him struck off. . .' The words and the tone were of a man used to authority. It didn't fit with Ben's role as a recluse of years.

'What would you do with the place if you had your way?' Ben asked her suddenly, as if diverting his anger into another channel. Laura hesitated and then smiled.

'Everything,' she said simply. 'All the things you've listed as being provided ought to be the right of our elderly, even if they can't afford it. Goodness knows, most of them have worked hard and paid taxes all their lives.' She hesitated. 'You know the thing I hate most about Sunset Lodge, though—the thing I'd change tomorrow if I had my way?'

'What?' She had his full attention.

'The name. Sunset Lodge. I loathe it. Why not just call it The End and be done with it? Some of the residents come in when they're in their late sixties and show every sign of staying until they're in their nineties. That's thirty years of sunset!'

Ben smiled. For the first time that night his smile lit his eyes and the deep black eyes softened. Laura looked up at him and caught herself on a gasp. She was like a moth attracted to the light. . . And, as if the light were too strong and she was afraid, she turned away, crossing to the little kitchenette to refill the kettle.

'No more coffee for me.' Ben had put his mug down on the coffee-table and was staring at Laura's turned figure. The cup below him was still three-quarters full. 'I have to get back.'

'To your sanctuary?' Laura turned and stared at him.

'Yes,' he said shortly.

'Do you really write murder mysteries?' Laura asked

curiously. To her delight, her words made his stern face break again into a smile. 'Now what have I said to make you laugh?'

'What on earth makes you think I write murder mysteries?' Ben demanded.

'My receptionist told me you do,' Laura explained. 'Rich recluses always write murder mysteries. If they're just recluses and not rich then they write obscure poetry.'

Ben gave a crack of laughter and Laura stared up at him. His face shed years of pain and unhappiness when he laughed. Why didn't he do it more often? she wondered. Had life treated him so unfairly?

'I don't write murder mysteries,' he was saying. 'And I can't imagine writing poetry. But I do write.' He shrugged. 'I write textbooks.'

'What sort of textbooks?'

'Medical textbooks.'

'Ohh. . .' Laura let her breath out on a long note of discovery. 'Ben Durell! Dr B. H. Durell, MB BS MSc FRCOG. Of course. Why didn't I recognise the name? You wrote our final-year obstetric text!'

'That's right.' He shrugged and the laughter faded. 'I must go,' he said brusquely.

'Back to the fortress?' Laura asked flippantly. She smiled. 'I'm sorry.' She looked down at Ben's knee and hesitated. 'You know, physiotherapy would help,' she said softly.

'Thank you, Dr Haley. I don't need advice.' Ben walked the few steps to the screen door and pulled it open.

Laura followed him. Ben had parked the truck only yards from her door. She stood on her front doorstep and watched as he walked around the truck.

Then she frowned. From the road beneath the
hospital came the sound of a vehicle being driven far
faster than was safe. There wasn't a siren. It wasn't an
ambulance or police car. As Laura listened she heard
the screech of tyres as the car took a bend at a wicked
pace. The motor screamed a protest and then the
vehicle was gunned harder up the hill.

Ben had heard it too. He stopped where he stood
and looked down the hill. Laura took a tentative step
down from the doorway so that she could see along the
road.

It was a big old panel van. It came around the bend
into the hospital car park, scattering gravel in all
directions, and pulled up at a crazy angle inches from
the casualty entrance. As Ben and Laura watched, a
young man jumped from the cab and ran into the
hospital.

Laura didn't hesitate. She hadn't had an emergency
since she had started work at Calua Bay, but it looked
as if she had one now. She reached the casualty
entrance as the man appeared again, towing a night
sister in his wake.

The entrance to Casualty was brilliantly lit. The man
pulled open the doors to the rear of the panel van,
allowing both Laura and the night nurse to see inside.

'It's my wife. . .' He was almost incoherent with
fright. 'She's. . .she's having a baby. . .'

Laura was already inside the van, bending over the
huddled figure on a mattress in the back.

The woman was young, in her early twenties, Laura
guessed and totally exhausted. Her eyes were blank
and distant with the vestiges of fear and pain, but she
had almost gone past that. Her face was two huge
pools of shadow surrounding the pain-filled eyes. As

Laura bent over her she didn't acknowledge her presence at all. Laura placed her hand on the girl's wrist and winced as she felt the faint, thready pulse.

'How long has she been in labour?' she snapped at the man. He was staring in at her in dumb misery.

'Since yesterday morning. She was going really well and then. . .and then it just sort of stopped. And now the baby's heartbeat is dropping. At least, it was before we left home.' He took a deep breath. 'It was down to seventy then. It's probably dead by now.'

Since yesterday morning. . . Laura turned and stared at the man. 'Why didn't you come in then?' she demanded.

'We. . .we don't believe in doctors.' His tone held the last traces of defiance. 'Not any more. I've done my nursing training and we wanted to have it at home.'

Laura turned back to the girl, her heart sinking as she did so. Laura wasn't trained in obstetrics. Calua Bay was too small to provide proper obstetric facilities, and the women went to one of the bigger centres across the mountains to give birth.

'Let's get her inside,' she snapped. Already there was a trolley in position. The charge sister was snapping orders to her underling with an urgency that matched Laura's own.

Three minutes later Laura was feeling sick with horror. She hadn't checked the baby's condition, but it no longer seemed to matter. It was the mother's life that was being threatened, and it was the mother who was Laura's first concern. She did a swift examination and her findings left her with nothing but dismay. The baby was in a posterior position, wedged fast with pronounced swelling caused by relentless, sustained pressure on the tiny head.

What on earth could she do to retrieve the situation? Laura glanced up at the girl's ashen face and moved swiftly to set up a drip. All the time her mind was racing.

There was no way she could get a live baby out of this. How on earth, though, was she going to deliver the baby at all?

She couldn't. She could put up a drip and if she was lucky—if the girl was lucky—she could replace fluids and keep shock at bay for long enough to keep the young mother alive on the trip inland. To manipulate the baby after this length of time. . . How the hell did you cope with such a presentation? It was the stuff a young doctor's nightmares were made of.

And then she lifted her head as a sudden faint hope flickered into her mind. The only time she had read of such presentations was in her student's textbook. And the man who had written the text might still be in the car park.

The drip was in position. It must have been the world's fastest insertion rate, she thought thankfully as it slid into position. Then, sending up a silent prayer that he hadn't left, she left Theatre, running swiftly outside and across the car park to Ben Durell's truck.

Ben was still there. The road into the hospital was double-car width but the panel van had blocked it completely with its unorthodox entry. Until it was moved, Ben couldn't leave.

'Dr Durell, I need your help.' Laura's voice was not quite steady as she spoke. She didn't yet know whether the baby was dead or alive but she knew that to save even the mother's life at this stage was probably beyond her skill. Swiftly she outlined what was happening.

Ben listened in silence. He was leaning against the bonnet of his truck, his face impassive in the gloom.

'I can't cope with this,' Laura confessed as she finished. 'It's beyond—far beyond—my training.'

Ben didn't move.

'I no longer practise,' he said.

Laura took a step back and looked at him with incredulity. 'What do you mean, you don't practise?' she demanded.

'Just what I said. I write textbooks. I don't practise.'

Laura took a deep breath. 'Well, I can't get that baby out,' she said harshly. 'The only way I know is to do a Caesar, and a Caesar with the baby in that position is beyond my skill even if I could do it on my own. It's a five-and-a-half-hour drive to the nearest specialist obstetrician, and if I send her like that I doubt if she'll be alive at the end of the journey.'

'Well, you chose to be the doctor here,' Ben said coldly. 'If you choose to practise when you haven't the skills needed I can't be held responsible.'

Laura gasped. She looked up at his cold, implacable face and felt her temper rising.

'I'm practising here because I'm all Calua Bay could get,' she said. 'Cliff Paige advertised for three months before I replied. Doctors hate remote postings. And I've never made any secret of my lack of obstetric training. I'm not skilled at obstetrics and neither is Cliff Paige. We advise all our mid patients to go to Canberra the fortnight before the baby is born. We do not advise them to come in to Calua Bay after thirty-six hours of prior labour!'

Ben had turned away. 'I haven't practised for five years,' he said quietly. 'I'm not about to start now. If you'll arrange for that van to be moved. . .'

Laura's breath drew in on a hiss of stunned anger. For a long moment she stared at him.

'Just a moment,' she whispered finally. Her voice was trembling with impotent rage. 'You can ask the driver to move it himself.'

She walked back over to the casualty entrance, her face ashen with anger. Inside, sitting numb and miserable on a waiting-room chair, was the father of the baby. Laura took him by the arm and motioned him to follow her.

'What's your name?' she asked gently, taking his arm and leading him across the car park.

The man followed, unresisting, shocked into compliance. The way he was at the moment, if someone had given him a pistol and told him to shoot himself in the foot he probably would have complied.

'Tom. . . Tom Burne. And my wife's name is Alice.'

'I need you to do a bit of persuasion for me,' Laura told him. She led him over until they reached Ben. Laura tilted her chin and stared straight at Ben.

'Ben, this is Tom Burne. I want you to explain to him why you won't make an effort to save his wife.'

Ben's face jerked up. He stared at Laura as though he hated her. 'Go to hell,' he said savagely.

'Dr Durell is a specialist,' Laura told Tom calmly. 'He's an obstetrician with skills to make all the difference in keeping Alice alive. But he won't use them because he thinks Alice might shrink from the sight of his scarred face. What do you think, Tom?'

The stunned man looked from one to the other, clearly at a loss. Laura didn't blame him. She was at a loss herself. This was Alice's only chance, though, and she had to take it.

Tom looked at Laura again, and then across to Ben.

'Is it true?' he whispered. 'Can you help Alice?'

'I. . .' Ben looked at the two faces turned to him and swore. 'That's blackmail,' he told Laura savagely.

'It is,' she agreed, her voice carefully expressionless. 'But I haven't a choice. And neither has Alice.'

He swore again and then turned to the truck. He hauled a box of files out and threw them at Laura and then lifted out the second box.

'What are you doing?' Laura asked, puzzled.

'Putting these damned files into safe-keeping,' Ben explained bitterly. 'If I'm in Theatre for hours I want these under lock and key.'

Three minutes later the precious files were in the hospital safe, and Ben and Laura were in Theatre. Tom was under the care of a ward maid, being fed hot sweet tea. He seemed almost as shocked as his wife. He might have nursing training, Laura reflected, but any vestige of that training had been shocked out of him.

Alice had been placed under the theatre lights. She was immobile and very close to unconsciousness. Laura checked her vital signs as Ben scrubbed.

Surely they were too late anyway, Laura thought to herself as she worked. The girl was so close to death. And the child. . .

They had to try. While the girl was breathing they had to try.

Then Ben was at the table, wincing at what he saw. He picked up a stethoscope and held it low on the girl's abdomen. As he listened his eyes widened.

'There's a live baby in here,' he said softly. 'Distressed, but still alive.'

The anger was suddenly gone from his face. As he administered a pudendal block there was no reluctance

or hesitation. Ben Durell might not have practised for
five years, but the role of specialist obstetrician was
still his. His orders came fast, and Laura and the two
nurses in Theatre ran.

He knew what to do. Laura drew in her breath in
amazement as she saw him lubricating and inserting
skilful fingers, feeling the position and the resistance.

Surely he can't deliver it normally? Laura thought.
It seemed, though, that it was just what he intended to
do.

'Have you Kjelland's forceps?' he snapped. Laura
looked a question to Sister Carter and the girl moved
to fetch them. There was always a full obstetric kit on
hand, just in case, though it was little use having
equipment none of the staff had the skills to use.

Then Ben was pressuring the baby back, easing the
tiny body into a changed position.

It was against anything Laura had ever been taught,
to go in opposition to the birth path. Alice's body,
though, had ceased its awful contractions. It was no
longer trying to expel the child, and Ben used its
temporary limpness to slide the baby away from the
outside world.

Laura would have said that Ben had large hands. His
fingers, though, were as delicate and skilful as the
world's greatest pianist. Carefully lubricated with
chlorhexidine, they felt and probed, moving a fraction
of an inch, exerting pressure and changing direction as
they felt resistance. He had all the patience in the
world. It was as if he didn't know that he had a
distressed baby and a dying mother.

There was nothing more for Laura to do. She had
picked up Alice's hand and was holding it, feeling the
thready pulse. Her own pulse must be near stopped,

she thought. She was afraid to breathe. Behind her she could sense the eyes of the two nurses, waiting with breath as tightly drawn as hers.

And then Ben's hands moved forward again as the baby changed position through the narrow pelvic bone. The forceps were in position for a mid-cavity rotation.

'Get a cloth,' Laura ordered one of the nurses. She motioned to Ben's brow, dripping with sweat, and the nurse moved in to clear his vision.

Ben's face was etched with strain, the scar on his cheek standing white on a pale background. He didn't acknowledge the nurse's ministrations. Then he swore savagely. As she glanced down, Laura's heart sank once again. With the easing of the pressure, the cord had moved down and been caught.

'Help me.' Ben's words were unnecessary. Laura knew what had to be done. Swiftly they moved the girl into position to ease the awful pressure on the baby's life-giving cord.

'General,' Ben snapped. 'Fast! And make it light, Dr Haley. This baby's had enough. I don't want it doped as well.' He flicked a glance down at the monitor showing the baby's heartbeat, and grimaced.

For a split-second Laura stared. To do a Caesarean. . . She opened her mouth to argue and then thought better of it. She was already moving to the anaesthetic trolley.

'Is the baby high enough?' she asked softly as the first needle was plunged home. In seconds the anaesthetic took effect, and, on Ben's signal, they moved the hapless girl again.

'It has to be.' Ben was already swabbing while a nurse cut away the girl's nightwear. 'As long as she doesn't spring another contraction on me. . .'

Then there was silence. Laura concentrated absolutely on the job at hand. To put a woman as close to death as Alice under general anaesthetic was a heavy risk and it would take all her skill. At least anaesthetics was an area she had concentrated on in the past. . .

And what of the baby? To do a Caesarean in such conditions with only two doctors. . . Laura flinched as she realised that there was little hope for the child. After such a delivery and with a prolapsed cord it would be born flat and lifeless, and neither Laura nor Ben could be spared to pay it any attention when it was delivered. Laura flicked her gaze to the junior of the two nurses.

'Is the humidicrib on?' she snapped.

'Yes.' The girl was retrieving instruments from the steriliser. 'I switched it on as soon as Mrs Burne arrived.'

'Good work,' Laura approved. She hesitated. 'You'd better get Meg in,' she said. Meg was the ward maid, but even an untrained pair of hands was better than nothing at the moment. At least the two sisters were competent. In a bush nursing hospital with only one doctor they had to be.

Thirty seconds later Meg came in, a big-boned, cheerful girl with a mop of bleached curls and a scared expression.

'Mrs Finlayson's not going to like this,' she said, trying for a grin. 'She's been nagging for cocoa for fifteen minutes.'

Laura had taken over Alice's breathing. She looked up at Ben and nodded. Mrs Finlayson's cocoa was just going to have to wait. Ben's scalpel moved and suddenly nothing else in the tiny room mattered. There was only Ben's hand.

It was the fastest Caesarean Laura had ever seen. Within seconds, it seemed, the scalpel was put aside. Ben's hands lowered through the incision, felt cautiously and emerged, dripping blood. In his hands lay a lifeless bundle. The baby.

He couldn't do anything about it. Below his hands, the wound was oozing blood. Laura looked across at the monitors and gritted her teeth. She increased the oxygen and adjusted the drip-flow rate to maximum.

'Hurry,' she said under her breath. She didn't need to say it aloud.

The dripping bundle was handed back to the waiting sister. Sister Carter moved from the table to the humidicrib and started working.

'Clear the airway first,' Laura instructed. 'With the sucker. Then breathe for it. Fast!'

The nurse was already doing so. Sister Carter was oblivious to everything else in the room, and with relief Laura remembered Cliff Paige's telling her that the woman's training had been done at the children's hospital.

There was nothing else to be done. Laura turned back to Alice, concentrating on the rise and fall of the pump.

Finally the wound was closed. Ben stood back, exhausted. 'OK,' he told Laura wearily. 'Reverse the anaesthetic.' And as he said the word another sound echoed around the room, making them turn and stare. It was the mewing cry of a new-born child.

Laura was still intent on the job at hand and had no time to react, but Ben turned as if he had been struck. He stared at the triumphant face of Sister Carter.

'Did I hear what I thought I heard?' he said softly.

Sister Carter didn't answer. Her smile said it all, and

the mewing started again, increasing in volume as the tiny new-born infant found his lungs.

'I think. . .' Sister Carter said softly. 'I think we might have a healthy little boy here. I think. . .' She took the thermal wrap from Meg's waiting hands and wrapped the little boy, and then offered him across to Ben.

It was as if the child were his own. For a moment Laura thought Ben was going to weep. He was a born obstetrician, Laura knew. The love of new life was still within this man, no matter how much he denied that he wished to continue practising. He cradled the child in his large hands with something approaching reverence. Then he lowered him on to the small side-table, unwrapped him swiftly and did a fast examination.

'I don't know how he did it,' Ben said slowly. 'But he's OK.' As the baby's wails increased in momentum he smiled. 'All right, young man,' he said softly. 'You want your mother, I guess.' He glanced back down to the table, where Laura was still working over the unconscious girl. 'She'll be with us in a moment.' He handed the baby back to Sister Carter to wrap and place in the humidicrib, and then came back to where Laura was watching Alice emerge from the anaesthetic.

It was as if, now her body had finally expelled the child, Alice had decided to live. The monitors were stabilising. Laura still watched like a hawk, but the girl was breathing for herself again, and the breathing was becoming deeper as Laura watched.

Ben moved below and started dressing the incision site, but his attention was still on the girl's face. He kept glancing up, waiting. And finally Alice opened her eyes.

For her the pain had stopped. Later there would be

pain from the tremendous battering her body had taken, but for now there was just exhaustion and relief. Her eyelids fluttered.

'Tom?' she whispered.

'We'll get him now for you,' Ben said quietly. He motioned to Sister Carter, who picked up the now sleeping infant and carried him over to the table. 'But first it's time you met your son. . .'

The girl's eyes opened wider. Ben took the bundle from Sister and lowered it so she could see the tiny face. And then Alice's eyes filled and she lifted her hands.

Ben gently placed the bundle beside her. The baby needed the warmth of his humidicrib, but that could wait. For now, Alice's need was greater.

Alice looked down in wonder at the tiny new life beside her. She touched her son gently on his cheek. And then she turned to Ben and raised her hands again. She grasped Ben's skilled hands in hers and looked at him through a mist of tears.

'I think we owe our lives to you,' she whispered. 'Thank you.'

Half an hour later they were finished. Alice Burne was sleeping, as was her new-born son. Tom's brother had materialised from the town and had taken Tom off for some sleep as well, and the hospital was settling down to its peaceful normality. Laura glanced at the clock above the sister's station. Twelve-thirty!

'Would you like to stay the night?' she asked Ben slowly as they walked towards the entrance. If he felt anything like as drained as she did he wouldn't be capable of the long drive home. 'My couch converts to a bed.'

'Thanks,' he said drily. 'If your couch is as comfortable as it looks I think I'd rather go home.' He hesitated. 'I could use coffee before the drive, though.'

'Of course.' Laura glanced up at him and then away. His face was drawn and weary, as if the strain of the past few hours had been almost too much to take. She felt a sudden almost compulsive urge to reach up and stroke away the lines of strain. And Ben. . . Suddenly Ben Durell was staring down at her as if almost willing her to do it.

'I'll get the files from the safe.' Ben broke the silence, speaking roughly, and Laura turned away.

'And I'll put the kettle on,' she responded. 'Come over when you're ready.'

Laura walked the few steps to her flat. There was a light that illuminated the path between the hospital entrance and her front door, but she didn't turn it on. The light shone on two ward windows, and Laura suspected that the hospital residents had been disturbed enough that night. It was impossible to have a drama such as the Burne birth in a small hospital without most of the patients' being aware of it.

As Laura reached her front door she stopped in surprise. The door was wide open. Laura frowned, and then her brow cleared. She had been standing in her entrance when the panel van had arrived. She must have left the door open in her haste. And Ben too must not have noticed the open door before she had called him away. Laura walked inside and flicked on the light.

The place had been ransacked. Her kitchen cupboards were wide open and the contents strewn on the floor. Furniture was upended and drawers tipped out. The whole flat was chaos. Laura's breath drew in on a gasp of horror.

Afterwards Laura told herself what she should have done. She should have turned and run, got herself out of the flat as fast as her legs would take her. Instead she ventured further in. In the bedroom a man stood back, hiding in the shadows.

Laura flicked on the light and entered the room. The shadows were now lit and there was no hiding-place. From beside the wardrobe a figure stepped out towards her.

And Laura recognised him. It was Craig Palmer. Laura had been introduced to him in her first week in the town, but when she had met him he had been an urbane, confident businessman, dapperly dressed in a three-piece suit. The transformation was almost ludicrous. This man was neither urbane nor confident. He looked desperate and out of control.

'Where are the files?' he asked softly. He took a swift step and grasped Laura's arm so tightly that she cried out. 'Where are the bloody files?'

'Ben. . . Dr Durell has them,' Laura whispered, almost too shocked to speak. 'He's. . .he's taken them home.'

'Lying bitch!' The intruder lifted a hand and struck her hard across the cheek. 'Ben Durell's truck is parked here and he's over in the hospital. I checked. I've searched the bloody truck and they're not there. Where the hell are the files?'

'They're not here,' Laura said desperately. 'We put them in the hospital safe.'

The man's eyes narrowed. His grip on her arm tightened. And then he looked up as he heard what Laura was also hearing—the sound of footsteps on gravel.

'What the. . .?' He swore and shoved Laura aside.

Then he reached down, and when his hand came up Laura saw the flash of a gun.

'Don't be stupid,' Laura whispered. 'You're in enough trouble already.'

'You can shut your face,' he told her. 'Now get out of my way.' He raised his arm and aimed towards the darkness of the doorway.

And then Laura screamed. She screamed as she had never screamed in her life before, and as she did she launched herself at the wickedly pointing gun.

The night spun round in a whirl of screaming and flailing arms. She felt herself scratching and kicking, holding on like a terrier with a rat.

It couldn't last. He overpowered her with ease. She felt herself being forced down on to her knees and, from a long way off, a blunt, hard instrument came crashing down on to her exposed head.

She knew nothing else. The night melted into pain, and then darkness, as the floor came up to meet her.

CHAPTER FOUR

LAURA woke to a white world. She opened her eyes and was hit by white. The whole world had turned white and it hurt. She closed her eyes in instinctive defence but it still hurt.

For a moment she lay back and did nothing, trying to summon enough courage to try again. Finally she allowed a chink of light to penetrate her eyelids. Slowly, slowly she lifted them completely.

The world wasn't completely white, but most of it was. The counterpane of the hospital bed was white, as were the walls, and the ceiling of the ward. Only the floral curtains and the stained wooden wardrobe showed Laura that her eyes were still seeing normally.

Her head hurt, as if she were clamped in a giant vice. Gingerly she raised her hand to her forehead and found a large soft wad taped in position. A bandage. . . She lay motionless on the high-piled pillows and let herself think, until the events of the night before came flooding back.

The gun. . . There was a gun. . . He was pointing it at. . .

'Ben!' she whispered fearfully as her mind filled with the panic of last night. She looked around in terror and found the bell. Grabbing it, she pushed the call button down hard.

It wasn't Ben who came. It was a nurse, smiling at her as the door opened.

Surely she wouldn't smile if Ben has been shot?

Laura thought wildly. Would she? And then the nurse reached her bed and Laura was scarcely able to ask the question.

'Ben?' she said again. Her voice didn't sound like her own.

'I'm glad you're finally back with us,' the nurse said gently. 'We were starting to worry.' She picked up Laura's wrist and looked down at her watch. Laura snatched back her wrist in frustration.

'Ben. . . Dr Durell. . .' she stuttered. 'What happened?'

'I'll let him know you're awake when I've taken your obs,' the nurse said soothingly, retrieving her wrist. 'We've sent him off to your flat for a sleep, but he insisted on being woken as soon as you came around.'

'He's OK?' Laura faltered.

'He's fine.' The nurse popped a thermometer under Laura's tongue. 'He's a bit tired, though. I gather it was some night.' She grinned. 'I was on duty yesterday afternoon. I left a nice, sleepy little hospital when I went home, and when I came back it was sleepy again. If it weren't for the presence of young Samuel Burne, who's making his presence felt in the nursery, and your bandaged head, I'd say the night staff had made it all up.'

Laura didn't answer. She couldn't. She was silenced effectively by the sliver of glass under her tongue.

Besides, her head hurt. It didn't really matter about anything else. As long as Ben was safe. . .

'You're sure he's OK?' she asked wearily as the thermometer came out.

'Who—Samuel?' the nurse smiled. 'He's fine. With a set of lungs like his, he's lording it over us all.' She hesitated and then looked across to the screened bed beside Laura. 'His mum's fine too. She's exhausted, but her obs are settling nicely.'

'I meant. . .' Laura bit her lip. 'I meant Dr Durell.'

'He's fine too,' the nurse reassured her. 'Just tired.'

It was beyond Laura to ask any more. She lay back on the pillows and closed her eyes. The nurse looked down at her sympathetically, and then lifted a glass of water to her lips.

'Drink just a little,' she encouraged. 'Then I'll let you be.'

Laura swallowed obediently, but she was already drifting back towards sleep.

She woke to the sound of voices. As she drifted out of sleep she didn't open her eyes immediately. The pain had receded. If she opened them it might come back. Then, as the deep, rough voice discussing the obs with the nurse penetrated her consciousness, her eyes opened involuntarily. Ben!

She looked up and found his eyes on hers. He was unshaven, his eyes were showing fatigue, but, as the nurse had assured her, he was unhurt.

'Good afternoon,' he said mildly as he saw her open her eyes.

Afternoon. . . Laura's eyes widened and she lifted her hand to see her watch. It was three-thirty.

'I've slept the day away,' she said in wonder.

'It's the best cure for split heads that I know,' Ben smiled. A bell rang somewhere close by and the nurse looked a question at Ben and then disappeared from his side. 'How does it feel?'

Laura considered. 'Sore,' she said at last. She winced as her fingers felt the bandage. 'Is it really split?'

'Fifteen stitches,' Ben said firmly. 'And you bled like

a stuck pig.' He grinned. 'All over my second-best jacket.'

'Oh, Ben,' Laura whispered. 'I'm sorry.'

'Don't be sorry,' he said cheerfully. 'I gather if you hadn't offered him your head I might have been bewailing a bullet hole in the same jacket. And my blood too,' he added thoughtfully. 'And as far as I'm concerned if I have to get blood on my jacket I'd much prefer it to belong to someone else.'

Laura gave a weak smile and closed her eyes again. 'What happened?' she asked.

Ben looked down at her for a long moment and then picked up her wrist. His long fingers felt lightly for her pulse, but he didn't time it.

'It was almost over by the time I got there,' he said gently. 'I heard you scream and got to the door as his gun came down on your head. He didn't have time to raise his arm again before I laid him out cold.'

Laura's eyes flew open. 'Oh, Ben,' she gasped. 'You didn't?'

'I couldn't see what the hell else there was to do,' Ben admitted. 'Besides. . .' he surveyed his bruised knuckles thoughtfully '. . . it did me good.'

'And where is he now?'

'Rotting in gaol, for all I care,' Ben said ruthlessly. 'By the time he came around I had him trussed up with a couple of pairs of your nylons. He'll live, unfortunately.'

Laura stayed silent. It could so nearly have been a tragedy. 'He must have been mad,' she whispered finally.

'Just stupid.' Ben pulled up a chair beside the bed and sat down. 'He's a small-time accountant, but in this town he thinks he's important. He and his wife

have been living high on the proceeds from Sunset
Lodge and have been getting greedier and greedier the
longer they got away with it. And suddenly I appeared,
and they knew their little system was going to be blown
apart. He knew he'd get gaol. His only hope was to
destroy the records. Without written proof it would be
all hearsay evidence and he'd probably just get off with
a bond. Not even that if he could persuade a few staff
members to lie for him.

'And then I played into his hands by not going home
immediately,' Ben continued. 'He broke into my truck
while we were in Theatre and then into your flat. And
when you came he panicked.'

'He certainly did.' Laura touched her bandaged head
ruefully. 'How bad is it.'

'Not too bad,' he reassured her. 'The cut runs around
your hairline and down behind your ear. It must have
been a fair whack he gave you, but you're lucky it
wasn't full front on the forehead. He could damn near
have killed you. As it is, you'll be left with just a faint
hairline scar.'

'I'll match you,' Laura said lightly.

He grinned and stood up. 'I don't think so.' He
stood looking down and then picked up her chart. 'Do
you want me to write you up for some pain-killers?'

Laura shook her head carefully. 'No.' She bit her
lip. The last thing she wanted to do was to get out of
this bed, but there was work to do. 'I need to get up,'
she said.

He shook his head. 'Tomorrow will be time enough,'
Ben said firmly. 'You'd be risking dizziness and a fall
today, and I don't want those stitches breaking.'

Laura looked up at him. 'But that means you're
trapped,' she said softly. She looked over to the bed

beside her, where Alice was still sleeping. The drips would still be running. There was a case for transferring Alice and the baby to Canberra, but the journey was the last thing the girl needed. However, she still needed competent medical attention, and now there was only Ben.

'I'm sorry,' she whispered to Ben. 'I didn't want to do this to you.'

Ben grinned down at her, the weariness showing through his smile.

'I know it's a set-up,' he assured her. 'Just a very clever ruse to get Ben Durell down from his mountain.'

'Will you stay down?' Laura asked softly.

Ben stood looking at her, the grin slowly fading. 'I'm pretty much attached to my mountain,' he said.

Laura slept for the remainder of the day, and most of the next. Gradually the throbbing of her head eased. On Sunday afternoon she ventured a walk out to the hospital sun-room and was amazed at how shaky her legs really were.

The hospital was a buzz of activity, livelier than Laura had ever seen it. There were reasons for that other than the fact that the hospital was full. News of Friday's events had filtered around the town. The place had gossiped about Ben Durell for years. Now he was in their midst and the townfolk didn't want to miss an opportunity to see the 'phantom' for themselves. Distant relatives were finding they had an urgent need to visit the hospital, and the patients hadn't realised they had so many friends.

Laura felt for him. She ran a clinic on Saturday and Sunday mornings for emergencies. Usually they amounted to four or five patients with trivial things such as earache or bad sunburn. When Laura glanced out of her window on Sunday morning she counted no less than twenty cars in the clinic car park.

If he was desperate to hide his scars, this was hardly the way to do it. Laura winced as she thought of the inspection the town gossips would be subjecting him to. But then, she thought, perhaps it was the only way for him to rejoin the human race; to be thrown in at the deep end.

On Sunday evening Laura asked the ward maid to fetch a dress and sandals from her flat. It was time to go home. She dressed slowly, Alice watching her in concern from the other bed.

'Should you be going so soon?' the girl asked shyly. 'Dr Durell hasn't said you can.'

'And that's from a girl who disapproves of doctors,' Laura smiled, and Alice had the grace to blush.

'They have their uses,' she admitted. She sighed. 'It was all going to be so wonderful. Tom and I have a little farm up behind the ridge and we've been struggling so hard to be self-sufficient. But nothing's working. Our veggies get bugs. The cockatoos and bell-birds eat our fruit. The dam's drying up and we have to cart water, and now this. . .' She fell silent and then looked at Laura. 'Believe it or not, we're both trained nurses. You'd think at least we would have been able to deliver a baby. All our training did, though, was make us super-confident right up to the point where our knowledge told us how much trouble we were in.'

'Why do you disapprove of doctors?' Laura asked quietly.

Alice shrugged. 'We just had too much of them, I guess,' she said. 'We were working in a high-tech coronary-care unit in Sydney and had to watch the

efforts made by doctors to keep alive patients who
were ready to die. We were so turned off in the end
that we decided to try the alternative.'

'No doctors at all,' Laura smiled. 'It's a bit of a
monumental leap.'

'I know,' Alice agreed. She looked down into the
crib at her side and smiled softly at her son. 'We're
going to have to rethink a few other things too,' she
said quietly. She bit her lip. 'The farm idea's hopeless.
It looks as if we're going to have to go back to Sydney.'

Laura looked sympathetically over at the tired girl
on the next bed. Swallowing ideals was hard medicine.
'At least you'll be taking a healthy little boy back with
you,' she said gently. 'Thanks to one of those doctors
of whom you disapprove. Dr Durell managed a
miracle.'

'Two of those doctors,' Alice corrected her. 'Tom
told me you bullied Dr Durell into helping.' She
grinned. 'Sam will enjoy being told the "phantom"
saved his life.'

'You've heard of Dr Durell?' Laura queried.

'Everybody has,' Alice said simply. 'I was expecting
to see an ogre with two heads.'

'And I've only got one and a half!' From the doorway
came Ben Durell's gravelly voice, and the girls spun
around in consternation. To their relief, though, Ben
was smiling. 'It's good to see you taking an interest in
the world,' he told Alice severely, 'even if it is just my
head-count.' And then he looked across at Laura.
'What the hell do you think you're doing?'

'Going home,' Laura said evenly. 'Is that all right
with you, Dr Durell?'

He shook his head. 'No,' he said shortly.

'Well, I'm sorry,' Laura responded. 'But I think I'm

fit.' She smiled up at him and echoed something he'd said to her days before. 'I can take care of myself. I haven't a medical degree for nothing.'

He drew in his breath and Laura waited for an explosion. She regarded him with interest. Finally he let out his breath and regarded her with resignation.

'OK,' he said, and a calculating smile had started behind his dark eyes. 'You're going to have to share your flat, though.'

'Share my flat. . .?' Laura frowned up at him. 'What do you mean?'

'Just what I said.'

'With whom?' Laura's voice was filled with foreboding. She knew the answer already. On the neighbouring bed, Alice watched with wide-eyed interest.

'With me, of course.' Ben looked down at the small hold-all beside the bed. 'Is this all you have?' He picked it up.

'Yes.' Laura sat down hard on the bed and stared at him. 'But I'm not going home with you.'

'Then you're not going home with anyone.' He smiled kindly at her. 'You know, you really would be better to stay here.'

'But I'm not sick.'

'You can't have it both ways,' Ben said placidly. With the hold-all in his hand, he limped out of the door.

The flat had been tidied. Laura stood at the front door and stared in, almost as if she was expecting Craig Palmer to still be there.

'It's fine, you know,' Ben said gently. He was standing behind her, waiting. 'Palmer's in gaol.'

'I know. . .' Laura's voice was unsteady. 'It still feels funny.'

'That's a normal reaction,' Ben told her. 'Your home is supposed to be a sanctuary. When it's violated like that it's a personal assault in itself. And you've been physically assaulted too.'

Laura walked slowly in and looked around. 'Did you clean it?' she asked.

'A couple of the nurses gave me a hand yesterday,' Ben admitted. 'And Tom Burne. He wanted to help.'

Laura picked up a photo from the bureau. It was a photograph of her parents taken years before. The glass had been smashed but the photograph was intact.

'Why did he do so much damage?' she said hesitantly.

Ben shook his head. 'I guess he had ideas of making it look like a normal robbery,' he said. He shrugged. 'Who knows? The man was unhinged.'

Laura stood staring down at the picture.

'Your parents?' Ben queried, following her gaze.

'Yes.'

'Are they still alive?'

Laura shook her head. 'I was a late baby. My father died when I was in my teens. My mother died two months ago.'

'Two months ago. . . Just before you applied for the job here.'

'Yes.' Laura put the photograph down with a bump, as if she was done with the conversation. Then she turned to the corner of the room where the divan stood.

It had been converted into a bed. A hospital mattress had been laid over its hard vinyl surface, and it was made up with hospial linen. Laura took a deep breath.

'So you really do intend staying?'

Ben walked over to the bedroom and put Laura's holdall inside the door.

'I don't see that I have a choice,' he said grimly. 'You've precipitated me back into practice, however temporary. I can't leave Alice with a drip still set up and no competent doctor on hand.'

Laura stood quite still. The colour drained from her face. 'No competent doctor?' she queried in a flat tone.

'No competent doctor,' Ben said firmly. 'Or did you intend taking over a full load as from tomorrow morning?' He looked across at her. 'For heaven's sake, woman, sit down before you pass out. You're as white as a sheet.'

Laura laughed shortly and sank into one of the room's armchairs. 'OK,' she said shortly. 'I thought you were questioning my skills.'

Ben looked down at her and then shrugged. Crossing to the kitchenette, he put the kettle on before answering.

'I'm not questioning your skills,' he said quietly. 'You did a damn good job in Theatre on Friday.'

Laura flushed. 'Not as impressive as you, Dr Durell.' She hesitated. 'Ben, why aren't you working?' she burst out. 'Your hands. . . I don't know when I've ever seen such skill. Surely you can't throw away skills like that—waste your life writing textbooks. . .?'

Ben didn't respond. He stayed with his back to her, making coffee, then brought out a mug and offered it to her. To Laura's surprise, he hadn't made one for himself.

'I have to go back over to the hospital,' he said briefly, choosing to ignore her outburst. 'Tom Burne wants to talk to me and I said I'd be free about now.'

'He's probably going to make you justify the Caesarean,' Laura smiled. 'Or demand to know why you had to use anaesthetic.'

'Probably.' Ben smiled but the smile didn't reach his eyes. Looking at him, Laura realised just how much of a strain he was under. Friday night must have been as stressful for Ben as it was for Laura. More, she thought ruefully. For at least some of it Laura had been unconscious and under no strain at all.

The strain, for Ben, wasn't over. For years he had been in seclusion, and the shock of being thrust again into the public limelight must be tiring in itself.

'Go to bed,' Ben was saying. 'I'll be back in an hour and I want to see you under the covers and asleep.'

'Yes, boss,' Laura smiled. She looked up at the tired face of Ben Durell and her heart gave a strange lurch. He was doing this for her. Hesitantly she put up a hand and touched his scarred cheek.

'Thank you,' she whispered.

For a long moment he stood looking down at her, his eyes blank and expressionless. Then his hand came up and caught hers, dragging her fingers away from the scarred surface of his cheek.

'Don't touch me,' he snapped. He dragged her hand down and turned away. 'And get into bed, Dr Haley. You're not fit to be on your feet.'

'No, sir,' Laura whispered. She was talking to herself. Ben had wheeled around and limped out of the flat, pulling the screen door shut with a sharp bang behind him.

Laura stood watching his retreating figure as he walked over the gravel towards the hospital. And as she watched she knew with absolute certainty what was happening to her.

'Oh, no,' she whispered to herself. 'I can't. . . It can't be happening again.'

CHAPTER FIVE

LAURA locked the door, undressed again and climbed into bed. Sleep wouldn't come. Her head was still aching, as were the bruises on her body, and the pillows seemed hard and unwelcoming. Finally she rose and crossed to the window, staring down across the valley to the sea.

Ben would be back soon. The seed that had settled in her heart burst and spread, filling her mind with panic.

She didn't want him here. She didn't want any man to come near her—to touch her heart and leave her open to the pain she had felt before. He had finched away at the touch of her fingers, as she flinched away from the filtering of his image into her heart.

She touched the wad of bandages at her hairline and winced. It hurt but at least it was a physical pain; a pain that would heal.

Below her, the valley slowly faded into dusk. As the light faded, the tiny pin-pricks of street- and house-lights flickered on. Finally, as the dusk deepened, the vast beacon beamed out across the sea from the lighthouse on Crag's Island, five miles off shore. It cast its silver path across the calm waters of Calua Bay.

I need to swim, Laura told herself. I need to get away—to walk, run, anything—just do something hard enough to drive away the demons. . .

The demons were still there, and the swim was something that would have to wait. She gave a fleeting smile at the thought of Ben's reaction if she immersed her stitches into salt water.

A knock on the door interrupted her thoughts. Laura hesitated fractionally before reaching for her robe and padding barefoot over the cool floor. Her heart had given a sickening lurch of fear.

Craig Palmer's in gaol, she told herself firmly. There's nothing to be afraid of. Even so, she opened the door only a crack and peered out before opening the door fully.

It was the man Laura had seen on the balcony the day she had first met Ben, the man Ben had addressed as Joe. He was standing on the doorstep bearing a computer and a worried look.

'Dr Durell said he'd be needing this.'

Laura stood aside and let the man enter. Joe cast her a doubtful glance before passing her and carrying the computer through to the kitchen bench.

'Is it OK here?'

Laura nodded.

'I've got a case with his shaving gear and some clothes. . .' Joe volunteered. He disappeared outside in a rush, like a nervous rabbit, and re-emerged bearing a small suitcase. Then he stood looking worriedly at Laura.

'Are you. . . Are you all right?' he ventured.

'Yes.' Laura wasn't feeling like being chatty. This man had been a boorish oaf the first time she had met him.

He knew it too. He stood there, his hands gripped together in front of him.

'I owe you an apology, I reckon,' he finally said. His voice was miserable. 'I was under orders. . .'

Laura relented and smiled. 'I know,' she told him. 'I'd imagine Dr Durell would be a hard boss.'

The man's face relaxed. 'Not really,' he admitted. 'It's only—he's had this bee in his bonnet about meeting people. "Keep people off the place," he told me. "Whatever else your duties are, that takes precedence."' Joe shrugged. 'But I shouldn't have been rude to the town doctor.'

'It's forgotten,' Laura said lightly. Then, as the man still hesitated, she said quietly, 'Is there anything else I can do for you?'

'No.' He grinned shyly and looked around. 'I just wanted to wish you luck. You're working a bloody miracle.'

'What do you mean?'

'I've been telling Ben Durell he's a fool any time these last few years.' He hesitated, frowning. 'When I first went to work for him his face did look awful,' he admitted. 'And he was getting a hard time. Something happened even after the accident—I don't know what—to make him shun everyone. But his face and his leg have been improving so much that there's been no need to be worried about people's reactions. It's taken your intervention, though, to make him look strangers in the face again.'

Laura looked curiously across at the little man in front of her. 'You're fond of him, aren't you?' she said quietly.

'Yes, I am,' he said bluntly. 'I was out of work when he met me. I was a timber cutter up in the bush behind the ridge until I had a heart attack. When Ben advertised for an odd-job man I was feeling that sorry for myself that I bloody near didn't apply. But now. . . I've been doing an accounting course by correspondence and I'm near to being fully qualified. And Ben's been paying me enough to support my wife and daughter while I've done it. All I had to do was odd jobs for him and protect him from the outside world.'

'You might be doing yourself out of a job by encouraging him out of his shell,' Laura said softly, and the man grinned.

'I used to worry about that,' he said wryly. 'But I heard a rumour yesterday about a local accounting practice that might be going cheap. It seems there's talk of Craig Palmer being otherwise occupied for quite some time.'

Laura laughed, her mood lightening. There was always a silver lining for someone.

'Well, good luck,' she told him.

'It's early days,' Joe warned. 'Besides, Ben hasn't sacked me yet.' He grinned. 'It's stupid to look forward to being sacked, isn't it?'

Laura nodded, smiling. And then she asked the question that had been in her mind since she had met Ben.

'What happened to him?' she asked quietly. 'How did he get the scars?'

Joe hesitated. 'He doesn't talk about it,' he admitted. 'All I know is what was in the papers at the time, six years ago. It was written up locally because the Durells had a holiday house up on the ridge even then. They were here every chance they could get. We considered them almost Calua Bay residents.'

'What was in the papers?'

'Their car was hit head-on by a petrol tanker on the road between here and Canberra. The driver of the tanker was high on amphetamines and overtook on a curve. There wasn't a damned thing Ben could do about it. He was lucky to get out alive, although I guess for a time he didn't think so.'

'His wife was killed outright?'

Joe nodded. 'There were three of them in the car. Ben, his wife and his wife's daughter by her first marriage. The little girl was about seven or eight. She escaped with minor injuries, but the front-seat occupants copped it.'

Laura frowned. So Ben had a stepdaughter. 'Where's his stepdaughter now?' she asked Joe.

He shrugged. 'I haven't a clue. Ben doesn't speak of her.' He shrugged again. 'Actually, it's not quite true,' he admitted. 'I know I post a cheque to an expensive ladies' college in Canberra every term.'

'So he's written off his stepdaughter as well as the rest of the world,' Laura said grimly. Then she looked up at Joe and smiled. 'I'm sorry. I had no business asking you questions like that.'

'And I had no business answering them,' Joe said frankly. 'But. . . Well, as I said, you seem to be working a miracle. And if you need a few facts to keep going it's not Joe McOnarchie who'll be standing in your way.'

'Thank you,' Laura said simply. She stood at the door and watched Joe climb into his car. She didn't move until the lights of the car disappeared down the hill. Then she turned her gaze back towards the hospital as she heard footsteps on the gravel. Ben.

'I thought I told you to stay in bed,' he said grimly. His limp was more pronounced and his eyes were cold.

'I had to let Joe in,' Laura excused herself. 'He brought your clothes and your computer.'

'Thank God for that.' Ben's hand came up and

stroked his unshaven chin. 'I was beginning to feel like a bushman instead of a doctor.'

Laura looked up at the dark stubble. 'I think a beard would suit you,' she commented.

'Do you just?' he grinned. 'I guess it would hide more of me. A paper bag over my head might be more effective.'

Laura laughed, but a corner of her mind acknowledged that Ben was only partly joking. Here it was again—the wish to hide himself from sight.

'How was Tom?' she asked. She crossed to an armchair and sat watching as Ben delved into his suitcase.

'Full of remorse,' Ben said briefly. 'He's had a hell of a fright. His training told him exactly what sort of mess they were in when the baby's heart-rate dropped, and it also told him to expect the worst. I don't think he can believe yet that he has a healthy baby and recovering wife.' He grinned. 'I'm glad it wasn't a little girl,' he said reflectively. 'I believe that in his present mood Tom would offer me her hand in marriage as well as half his kingdom.'

'It doesn't sound like much of a kingdom,' Laura said. 'From what Alice says, they're going to have to return to Sydney.'

Ben shook his head. 'No.'

'What do you mean, no?' Laura demanded.

'If I have to stay off my mountain for the next few days I'm going to have to sort out as many problems as I can while I'm down here,' Ben said shortly. 'Tom seems to me like a thoroughly competent nurse, who's disenchanted with mainstream medicine. I offered him the job of taking over Sunset Lodge.'

Laura gasped. 'Just like that?'

'Just like that.'

'I'm the medical director of the place,' Laura snapped. 'You don't think you should have consulted me first?'

'It's not your place to argue with the owner.' Ben opened a toilet case and examined its contents. Then he looked up and met Laura's angry look. 'You'll agree with me,' he said briefly. 'The man's too good to let slip through our fingers. He'll be a breath of fresh air in the place, especially if, as I suspect will happen, Alice becomes involved too. And one thing he won't be doing is overdosing his patients on sleeping drugs.'

Ben walked over to the bathroom door, and then stopped, looking back at her.

'I want you back in bed.'

'I'll go in a minute.' Laura was still angry. Surely she should have been consulted?

'Well, I'm taking a shower now,' Ben threatened her. 'And if you aren't under covers by the time I come out I'll pick you up and carry you there.'

Laura lay between the sheets and listened to the sounds of Ben in the bathroom. It was weird having a man in her apartment. Even Ross had never stayed. . .

He had never stayed because her mother was always there. Laura's mother wouldn't have minded in the least—would not have even noticed, but Ross had wanted Laura to himself. Or not at all.

Well, Laura had made the choice. It was funny, she thought, lying back on her pillows. Suddenly it was starting to seem clear-cut, as though she had reached the right decision after all. Was that because of Ben? Because the image of Ben's black eyes were superimposed on the memory of Ross's blue ones?

Laura gave herself an angry shrug and closed her

eyes. It was stupid letting herself think like that. There was no joy in turning to a man who had rejected the human race, much less her.

Ben had even rejected his stepdaughter. Laura turned this over and over in her mind. Her heart went out to the little girl. To lose her mother and then have Ben turn away from her. . .

She didn't know the facts, Laura reminded herself. And yet she knew that Ben didn't see the girl. Why?

'He wasn't her real father,' Laura whispered to herself in the night. 'Perhaps she has other family. . .'

The thought didn't comfort her. The image of a motherless little girl stayed with her.

Sleep wouldn't come. Laura lay and stared into the dark, listening to the faint noises from the next room. Her head was heavy on her pillows, but the consciousness of Ben Durell's presence was too strong. She listened to the sound of the computer keyboard. Ben was obviously not going to let himself fall behind his writing schedule by staying here. It went on for an hour or more. Then there was the sound of the kettle being filled and footsteps across the sitting-room, and Laura's door opened an inch.

'Asleep?' It was hardly above a whisper.

'No.'

'Cocoa?'

Laura smiled to herself. The great Ben Durell offering cocoa. . . He had come a long way in two days.

'Yes, please.'

A moment later the door opened to full width and Ben came in bearing two steaming mugs. He waited until Laura had struggled into a sitting position before handing one over, then sat down himself on the end of her bed. Laura took an appreciative sip.

'Thank you.'

'Can't sleep?'

She shook her head. 'I must be getting better. Besides, I've slept all weekend.'

They sat in silence. The room was warm, with the curtains moving softly in the balmy night breeze. The smell of the sea was everywhere. Outside, the moon was full, casting shards of silvery light across the two people in the room. Ben hadn't turned the light on when he entered. There was no need.

Finally Laura finished and Ben took her cup from her and stood up. There still seemed nothing to say. A thin, tense current ran between them, making each intensely aware of the other.

'Do you need anything else?' Ben asked finally, and Laura shook her head.

'No,' she told him. 'I should sleep now.'

He nodded and walked out of the room.

Contrary to her expectations, Laura did fall asleep. Her bruised body required it. For the first few hours she slept deeply, but, as the dawn neared, her sleep became shallower and she started to dream.

The horror of Friday night was still with her. In her dreams Craig Palmer was back again. He was holding his gun, pointing it straight at her heart. And besides him were the ghosts. There was Ross and there was her mother, standing side by side, and they too had guns. It was surreal, and yet for Laura it was reality. She couldn't escape. The guns gleamed with the cold, polished silver of heavy, deadly metal.

And then the dream deepened. In slow motion their arms were upraised and the guns were lined up, pointing at her. They were all staring at her, their eyes accusing and unyielding, each demanding something she couldn't give.

And then Ben was walking through the door and the guns were exploding, but it was not Laura who crumpled and fell. It was Ben, and the guns were firing over and over again. . .

'Ben! Ben. . .!' She was screaming into the night. 'Ross, no. Leave him alone. Ross! No!' The other figures faded. There was Ross and Ben, and Ross's face was contorted with laughter, while Ben's was twisted with pain.

And then the vision was cut off. Strong arms seized her and held her, pulling her into a haven of comfort and safety.

'Laura, wake up! You're dreaming, Laura.' The voice deepened until it was a harsh command. 'Wake up, Laura. It's a nightmare, that's all. There's nothing to be afraid of.'

The terror was still there. It clamped around Laura's heart, making her feel faint and sick. She clung to Ben as if she were drowning, trying to control the tremors sweeping through her body.

Ben's hold didn't slacken. It was the hold of a parent comforting a terrified child. He stroked her hair and waited for the shaking sobs to subside, his presence giving reassurance as nothing else could. And finally the tremors eased and the horror dissipated into the night. Laura was left feeling shaken and empty, and more than a little foolish.

'I'm. . . I'm sorry. I. . . Did I wake you?' Still his arms held her against him and she didn't move away.

'I should think so!' Ben looked down at her head, cradled against his chest in the faint tinge of dawn. 'I thought at the very least we had twenty rapists queued at your bedroom window.'

Laura gave a shaky laugh and pulled herself slightly away from him. 'It. . .it was very brave of you to come to the rescue, then,' she managed.

'I checked first,' he admitted. 'I opened the door half an inch just to count my opponents. Any more than two small ones and I was off to get help.'

Laura giggled and the terror receded further. She looked up at him and smiled shyly. 'Thank you,' she said simply.

And then, suddenly, the current between them changed. The warmth and the comfort had been replaced by something more. Ben was staring at her as if he had never seen her before, and Laura couldn't lower her eyes.

It was as if their gazes were locked together by a force stronger than both of them. Laura felt her heart move within her. His eyes, his hands, the feel of him and the first, faint hinting of the dawn; together they were a conspiracy holding her to him. She raised her lips mutely to be kissed.

Ben Durell needed to be inhuman to resist the invitation. In the faint dawn light he had never seen a woman more lovely than the girl in his arms. Laura's skin was almost translucent, and her huge dark eyes were shadows in her lovely face. The sheer silk fabric of her gown accentuated the curves of her ripe body, and he could feel its warmth under his hands. Only the white bandage against her forehead marred her perfection, but its presence was only adding to her air of fragility and helplessness.

Slowly, slowly, almost as if he was afraid, Ben brought his mouth down to meet hers.

The first kiss was a feather touch, as if both were unsure. Then Ben drew back, his eyes dark and fathomless in the dim light. Laura watched him, waiting, her eyes a question. She was sinking into a strong, warm current, and she knew she would not fight it. She couldn't. Her body was warm, and safe, and totally committed to the man in whose arms she was held.

It was as if Ben was fighting with himself. His face reflected a man at war with an inner barrier. It was as if he was still in pain, Laura thought. Slowly she brought a finger up and traced the outline of the scar on his face. This time he didn't flinch. And, as her finger reached the base of the scar where his mouth stretched into a tight line of struggle, the pain, for Ben, became too much. With a groan, his arms gathered her to him and she melted upwards to meet him.

This time the kiss was that of lovers. Their mouths entwined, his lips holding hers to him, demanding a possession that she granted with joy. It was as if she had been starved, she thought. His tongue entered her mouth, exporing her even white teeth and tasting her pleasure. Laura's lips opened joyfully. Her mind had screamed a final protest at Ben's first kiss and had then been stilled. It wasn't her mind that wanted Ben Durell. It was her body, and her body was in the ascendancy.

Ben's hands moved to hold her closer. His fingers cupped the rounded fullness of her breasts under the flimsy fabric of her gown, and Laura felt her breasts firm and swell in response. Her nipples were proudly erect, and Ben's probing fingers felt their message. Still their lips stayed locked together, and Laura's small tongue moved to do its own investigation. Her body moved to the touch of his hands, and, deep within her thighs, a tiny flame kindled and grew.

Who was this man who could do such things to her? She neither knew or cared. For the moment all that mattered was that he was here, and the pain and loneliness of the past few years had been driven away.

For how long he was here was also something she didn't know. It didn't seem to matter. All that mattered was here and now. All that mattered was that those hands keep moving, sending her senses to a quivering ecstasy of expectation.

She put her hands up to cup Ben's face and felt his body move in response. He wanted her as much as she wanted him. She could feel it and her body triumphed in it. There was only Ben.

Somehow the translucent fabric of her nightgown was lifted away. She felt it brush softly against her face before it floated unnoticed to the floor. Then Ben's hands moved again, glorying in the feel of her flawless skin, and Laura's body cried out in need.

'Ben. . .' From a long way she heard her urgent whisper. 'Oh, Ben. . .'

The words caught him and his hands stilled. And somewhere in that briefest of moments the world caught up with him.

Ben's mouth left hers. For a fraction of a moment he remained motionless, and then with an oath she was thrust back on to the bedclothes. He rose and stepped backward from the bed.

Laura lay in the half-dark, watching with eyes that reflected confusion.

'What's wrong?' she asked softly. She put a hand down and pulled up the sheet to cover her nakedness.

That he should stop, that he should leave her now was unthinkable.

'What the hell are you doing to me?' His voice was low and shaken. 'I don't want this.'

Laura's breath was drawn in on a tiny gasp. Did he think she was trying to seduce him? 'I. . . I. . .' Nothing came out. Words wouldn't come. She lay staring up at his accusing face.

'Who's Ross?' Ben asked heavily, taking another step backwards.

'My fiancé. . .'

'Your fiancé!' He said the word almost under his breath, but it echoed around and around the room.

'Not. . .not any more,' Laura said hastily. 'I. . . We broke the engagement off before I came here.'

'I see.' Ben's voice was harsh again and his words expressionless. And Laura knew that he saw nothing. He understood nothing. 'So you need someone to take his place?'

Laura drew in her breath again and a tiny thread of anger twisted around her heart. She looked up at the man above her and saw a stranger. He knew nothing about her, and didn't want to know. What on earth was she doing, allowing him to touch her, to kiss her and to be close to her?

'I don't want anyone to take Ross's place,' she said in a tiny voice.

'So what are you letting me kiss you for?' Ben was goading her. It was as if he was forcing anger on himself, driving himself to reject her.

Laura put a hand to her head in a forlorn little gesture that, had she known it, nearly had Ben back to the bed. . .back to her. She closed her eyes.

'Please get out of my bedroom,' she said tremulously. 'Now.'

There was a long moment of absolute silence. Laura wouldn't look. She couldn't. Then footsteps sounded across the bare floorboards. A door opened and banged closed again. When Laura finally opened her eyes, Ben was gone.

There was no more sleep to be had that night. Laura lay wide-eyed, watching the dawn gradually light the bare little room.

Her body still trembled from Ben's touch. She couldn't believe she had let him touch her. Laura had made herself a solemn pledge never to let another man near her, and to devote herself entirely to her medicine for the rest of her life. And now here she was, letting her defences crumble when the first presentable male came within her orbit.

Ben Durell was no ordinary male, she told herself firmly. Ben Durell was like no man she had ever met before. And if Laura had demons driving her then Ben had more of them. A dead wife, an alienated stepdaughter and a scarred body. . .

It was too much. Laura's bruised body couldn't take it all in. If I hadn't been hurt I wouldn't have let him near me, she told herself firmly. It's only that the attack on Friday night has left me feeling vulnerable. I don't really want anything to do with Ben Durell.

Her words wafted around and around in her head, but, try as she might, she couldn't make them sound sincere.

Finally the sound of the telephone shrilled through the flat. Laura rose, slipped on her robe and padded out to answer it.

Ben was before her. He was dressed, she discovered, and the remains of tea and toast were on the kitchen bench. By the time Laura emerged Ben had lifted the receiver and was talking into it.

'How long ago?' His voice was clipped and professional, and Laura knew at once it was a work call. She stood quietly while Ben made hasty notes on the pad beside the phone. Finally he put the phone down and turned to Laura.

'A car's gone over the embankment three miles south of the town,' he said briefly. 'The ambulance is on its way but the police think it's going to take a while to get the driver out. They want me to go to the scene.'

Laura nodded slowly. 'They don't want me to go?'

'I don't think they care either way,' Ben said shortly. 'But you're not driving. Where's your bag?'

'In the back of my car.'

'Keys?' he demanded.

Laura motioned to the hook beside the phone, and Ben lifted the keys off and walked to the door.

'Don't start surgery before I'm back,' he said shortly. 'It won't hurt them to wait. Get back to bed.'

'Yes, Doctor.'

She might as well have saved her breath. Laura's mock-subservience was wasted on an empty doorway. Ben had gone.

Laura didn't go back to bed. She showered and dressed, and made herself breakfast. Afterwards she cleaned up and sat looking through her windows down to the sea.

It seemed, whether she liked it or not, that she had a partner. On one level she was profoundly grateful. To have coped with road trauma this morning before a crammed day at the surgery would have stretched her capabilities to past their limit. On another level, though, she was worried. How long did the man intend to stay?

She looked across at his tumbled bed, left unmade in his haste to leave. Grimacing, she crossed the room to make it up for him, and as she did she recognised the faint masculine odour of his body. It caught her in a wave of physical awareness and her body responded with recogntion of the same signals it had been receiving the night before.

For a moment she was caught in blind panic. What was happening to her? This wasn't cool, calm Dr Laura Haley, career woman. This was some teenage schoolgirl, caught in an obsessive crush.

She had to get out of the flat or she would go mad. Laura glanced at her watch. Surgery was due to start in an hour. If she hurried she could get all the work out of the way at the hospital before that time.

Ben's words echoed faintly in her ears and she shrugged. The man was awfully fond of throwing his weight about, she thought ruefully. Well, she felt better, and it seemed stupid to sit here letting the work stockpile against Ben's return.

She had a second cup of tea and then checked her neat appearance in the long mirror in the bedroom. She was still pale. A little blusher would fix that. The bandage on her forehead was less easy to disguise, and Laura knew she would be hearing comments on it all day. Still, there was no help for it. It was either that or sit on her backside and let herself think about Ben.

With a decisive nod to her reflection she flicked back her flame-red hair and pulled her white coat over her dress. Dr Laura Haley was back in business.

CHAPTER SIX

LAURA did a leisurely ward-round, noting as she went that Ben had taken his role as stand-in doctor over the weekend seriously. The patients' medication was up to date, and, in some cases, thoughtfully changed to accommodate their improving conditions.

'Where's that nice Dr Durell?' old Mrs Finlayson grizzled to Laura. 'He was so understanding yesterday. No offence, dear.' She patted Laura's hand kindly. 'But there is something. . .well. . .something so much more competent about a male doctor.'

'Isn't there just?' Laura agreed through gritted teeth. She looked down at Mrs Finlayson's deceptively innocent eyes and smiled. Mrs Finlayson was a long-term patient with a broken pelvis, and had done nothing but find fault with Laura and the hospital staff since she was admitted.

'I'll tell you what,' Laura continued. 'If Dr Durell agrees we could transfer your care to him entirely.'

'That would be lovely,' Mrs Finlayson beamed. 'He's a specialist, you know,' she told the nurse standing behind Laura. 'So understanding. . .' She cast a covert look up at Laura. 'You're sure you don't mind, lass?'

Laura replaced the chart on the hook on the end of the bed and met the old conniving eyes.

'Mrs Finlayson,' she said, 'to keep all the patients in this hospital entirely to myself would be selfish on my part. And, believe me, the opportunity to share a chosen few would be pure pleasure.' She walked out before the old lady could digest her words, and the nurse at her side closed the door with a chuckle.

'You'll never talk Dr Durell into taking her on,' she grinned at Laura. 'As soon as you're fit he'll be back in his refuge like a shot.' She grinned again. 'Come to think of it, if I was threatened with the devotion of Mrs Finlayson I'd be there ahead of him.' A bell sounded two doors away, and the nurse went off down the corridor, still chuckling.

In the next room Alice lay cradling her baby. She looked up as Laura entered and smiled shyly.

'I'm glad you're feeling better,' she ventured.

Laura crossed to pick up Alice's chart and smiled. 'I could say the same for you. This is terrific. If Dr Durell OKs it we'll take the drip down this morning.'

'I. . . Aren't you my doctor?' Alice hesitated. 'I know he's a specialist, and I'm really grateful, especially now he's offered Tom the job, but I really would prefer you. . .'

'Because I'm a woman?' Laura asked curiously, and Alice gave a relieved smile.

'Yes,' she said simply. 'I know it's stupid; it's just that the examinations—well, they're so personal. . .'

Laura smiled. 'Thank you.' She replaced the chart and pulled back the bedclothes to check Alice's tummy. 'You have now cancelled out Mrs Finlayson, who thinks just the opposite. Nevertheless,' she added, 'I'm not removing the drip without Dr Durell's say-so. If we've specialist advice on hand we'd be foolish to ignore it.'

'Where is he?' Alice asked. The baby at her side gave an indignant wriggle as his mother moved.

'At an accident.' Laura frowned. Ben should have been back by now.

After Alice there was one more patient, and then Laura made her way to the sister's station.

'Any word from the ambulance?'

The sister in charge shook her head. 'Do you want me to contact them?'

Laura nodded and then stood silently waiting while the sister tried to make contact on the radio.

It took several minutes, which meant the driver was away from his cab, and when he finally responded he sounded harried. Laura signalled to the sister, and took the receiver herself.

'What's happening, Larry?'

'We've a fair mess here, Doc, and that's for sure. The driver's stuck in a wrecked car. The fire brigade are here and they're just setting up Jaws of Life now.'

Laura nodded to herself. 'Jaws of Life' was an impressive set of equipment designed for just such an eventuality. It literally cut open a car from any angle.

'How's the driver?' Laura asked.

'No good.' Laura could hear the pessimism in the man's voice. 'Doc Durell's doing all he can, but I dunno. . .' He hesitated. 'There's a girl here needs treating, but she won't leave until the boyfriend's free. Just lacerations, but some of them are pretty deep.' His voice grew more morose. 'Making a fair mess of the cab, she is.'

Laura smiled. The ambulance boys were notorious for their pernickety cleaning of the cab. 'Poor girl,' she said. She hesitated. 'Let me know when you're on your way in,' she said. 'I'll have Theatre ready.'

'Could be another half-hour,' she was told. 'We're going to have to go in through the back.'

Laura replaced the receiver, her face set in a grim

line. This was no minor road trauma. Ben was surely
having an initiation by fire back into medical life.

She gave instructions as to what she wanted in the
theatre, her mind clicking over the likely needs.

'You'd better contact a few of our regular blood
donors too,' she told the sister in charge. 'Have them
on stand-by, just in case.'

The sister nodded and bustled off.

Left alone, Laura wandered across to the clinic. Her
head was beginning to throb, but already patients were
arriving. Kylie was in Reception and greeted Laura
with caution.

'You look awful,' she told Laura frankly.

'Gee, thanks.' Laura dredged up a grin. 'How was
your weekend?'

'Not a patch on yours, by the sound of it.' She
smiled. 'Actually I had a smashing weekend.'

Laura raised her eyebrows. 'The life-saver?'

'He's not a life-saver,' Kylie told Laura for the
second time, her voice rising in defence. Laura
laughed.

'I know, I know. He's a very intelligent law student,
with impeccable taste in women.' She picked up the
first card. 'Who have you got for me?'

'Half the town, it seems,' Kylie retorted. 'They're all
dying to see Dr Durell.'

'Well, too bad,' Laura said quietly, staring around at
the sea of faces in the waiting-room. 'They're just going
to be stuck with me.'

'At least your bandage looks interesting,' Kylie said
cheerfully. 'That'll give them something to talk about.'
She wrinkled her nose. 'You're awfully white too,' she
observed. 'If you could manage to pass out we'd really
do as well as if we had Dr Durell here.'

'I'll see what I can do,' Laura said grimly. Then as Kylie gave a giggle she held up a warning finger. 'The way I'm feeling, smelling salts may well be the order of the day.'

If Laura had had time to think, she would have admitted to feeling awful and gone home to bed. As it was, she sat and listened to one trivial complaint after another, reflecting as she did so that no one seemed any worse than her. When the town's resident Nosy Parker, a woman who had been in twice on the previous week complaining of trivia, sat down and started a diatribe on how bad her headache was Laura could have cheerfully thrown something at her. She forced herself to listen attentively, though. It was on days like this that she was likely to miss something. To miss diagnosing a cerebral haemorrhage just because she had a headache herself would be unforgivable.

Mrs Thomas had no such thing, and Laura was finally rid of her. Her place was taken immediately by someone with something equally trivial. When she was halfway through listening to yet another list of symptoms, Kylie rang.

'The ambulance is on its way in, Dr Haley,' she apologised. 'You asked me to let you know.'

Laura looked down at the cards on her desk. She was three patients behind already. It couldn't be helped. She just had to cross her fingers that there was nothing urgent in the queue.

She finished writing a script for Mrs Leyland's fungal cream, then walked out through the waiting-room to the door beyond. As she did she sensed rather than heard the collective groans behind her as those waiting realised that the wait was going to extend indefinitely.

The ambulance was pulling into the entrance as Laura emerged. Sister Carter was at the entrance to Casualty, locking the doors wide open, and Laura breathed a sigh of relief at the sight of her. The girl exuded competence, and in situations like this good nursing staff were a godsend. Laura walked briskly over the gravel to the ambulance and stood waiting as the stretcher emerged.

The boy was still alive, but only just. Ben stepped down behind the stretcher, and at the sight of him Laura's breath came in as a gasp. He looked almost as shocked as the patients. Ben was holding a drip vertically above the stretcher and when he saw Laura he motioned behind.

'See to her,' she said brusquely. 'Then I need you in Theatre.'

Laura looked down at the extent of the boy's injuries.

'Surely he should go to Canberra,' she said quietly, and Ben nodded.

'We need to establish an airway first,' he said. 'He'll never make it like this.' The ambulancemen were already moving with their patient, and Ben moved inside with them.

Laura and Sister Carter were left to help the girl down from the back of the ambulance. Given a different scenario, she too would be carried, Laura thought grimly as she helped the girl down. The lacerations she had suffered looked ugly, and she was obviously deeply shocked.

'Get a wheelchair,' Laura said urgently. In moments Sister was back and the girl was helped carefully into the chair.

There was little Laura could do at the moment for

Relax with **FOUR FREE** Romances plus two Free gifts

Whatever the weather a Mills & Boon Romance provides an escape to relaxation and enjoyment. And as a special introductory offer we'll send you four FREE Romances plus our Cuddly Teddy and a Mystery Gift when you complete and return this card. We'll also reserve you a subscription to our Reader Service which means you could go on to enjoy :

- ◆ **SIX BRAND NEW ROMANCES** sent direct to your door each month.

- ◆ **NO EXTRA CHARGES** free postage and packing.

- ◆ **OUR FREE MONTHLY NEWSLETTER** packed with competitions (with prizes such as televisions and free subscriptions), exclusive offers, horoscopes and much more.

- ◆ **HELPFUL FRIENDLY SERVICE** from our Customer Care team on 081-684-2141.

> **Turn over to claim your Free Romances, Free Cuddly Teddy and Mystery Gift.**

Plus a FREE cuddly teddy and special mystery gift.

the girl. Ben would need her in Theatre. The girl was shaking uncontrollably. They put her into a bed in Casualty and Laura set up a drip.

'Turn up the heating,' she told Sister. 'I want her warm.' She turned to go, but as she did the girl's hand came out and clutched her coat.

'He is going to be all right?' she pleaded. 'Chris. . . My boyfriend. . . He is going to make it? He looks awful. . .'

Laura took the girl's hand and gripped it hard. 'I don't know,' she told her honestly. 'Between us, though, Dr Durell and I are going to give it our best shot.'

As she walked down the corridor towards Theatre she reflected on her words. 'Dr Durell and I. . .' How would she have coped if she had been on her own?

She wouldn't have coped at all, she acknowledged honestly. Not for the first time, she wondered how Cliff Paige had ever run this practice on his own.

In Theatre, Ben was already scrubbing, and Laura moved swiftly to her position beside the anaesthetic trolley. For the moment all other thoughts had to be put aside. There was only room for one thing, and that was to keep this boy alive while Ben carried out his repair work.

Ben cast her a worried look as he approached the table.

'Are you OK, Dr Haley? You don't intend passing out, do you?'

Laura flushed angrily and then remembered her head. Fifteen minutes ago it had been throbbing and she had been all too aware of it. Now it was as if it had never happened. The pain also had been thrust aside with the urgency of the case before them.

She cast Ben an irritable nod before bending over the trolley to make her preparations. She had no need to be reminded of it.

For the next twenty minutes there was almost complete silence in the room. Ben was not a surgeon but he had surgeon's fingers, Laura thought as she glanced at his work. She had little time to admire it, though. Her own job of keeping breath flowing into the injured boy's lungs was more than enough to hold her entire attention.

Finally they had done as much as they could do. It was far too soon to tell whether their efforts would be rewarded. There might well be internal injuries that could kill him. All they knew was that he could breathe. From here on he needed surgeons and equipment far beyond Calua Bay's scope.

'I want you to go with him to Canberra,' Ben said brusquely as he stepped back from the table. Laura looked up in astonishment. That a doctor needed to accompany the ambulance she had never doubted, but she had assumed she could persuade Ben. After all, there was so much work to be done here. . .

'I can't,' Laura said briefly. She cast a doubtful look down at the boy's shattered face.

'You haven't a choice,' Ben was saying. 'You shouldn't be working at all. You're dead on your feet and I'm damned if I'm going to take off for Canberra and leave you with a work-load that'd make two doctors flinch. At least this way you'll get some rest.' He turned to the wash-basins. 'And I don't want you back, either.'

'What do you mean, you don't want me back?'

'You're to take the rest of the week off. I'll cover for you and you can catch the bus back on Saturday.'

'You!' Laura was staring at him but she was ignored. 'But I can't leave——'

'You have to.' Ben shook his head. 'I know it's dangerous, leaving the hospital with only one doctor, but the medical set-up in this place is crazy. Cliff Paige needs a kick right where it hurts most.' His mouth set in a grim line. 'And I might be just the man to give it to him.' He motioned to their unconscious patient. 'Go and pack. I'll watch here.'

Laura stared at Ben and slowly shook her head. 'That's crazy,' she said softly. 'I'm not going.'

'Well, neither am I,' Ben said briefly. 'So, if you don't go, he'll die.'

'Well, I'm coming back with the ambulance, then,' Laura said desperately. 'I don't need time off.'

'You do, you know,' Ben said equitably. 'You've been battered and bruised, and you've had the fright of your life. Go shopping, take in a movie or two and get some sleep.' He hesitated and then grinned. 'Besides, I've had enough of sleeping on that singularly uncomfortable vinyl settee in your flat. For the next five nights I'm sleeping in your bed, whether you're there or not.'

Laura stared at him in stupefaction.

'Close your mouth, there's a good girl,' Ben advised kindly. He looked down at the boy beneath him, and moved to adjust a drip. 'Now go, Dr Haley,' he ordered. 'You're wasting time and our patient hasn't a lot of it to spare.'

Laura packed mechanically, throwing things into a small suitcase with no real thought for whether she needed them or not. Outside the door of the flat she was aware of the ambulancemen preparing the ambulance for the long trip over the mountains. It would be no easy ride, Laura knew, but she also knew that physically it would be less demanding than staying here.

What on earth had she let Ben Durell in for? Not for the first time she felt a surge of guilt. It was as if she had dragged him forcibly out of his shell and then refused to let him return. And now she was abandoning him to a job that was hers.

If only her body didn't ache so much. Ben was right. She did need time to recover. She lifted a couple of her favourite dresses from their hangers, laid them in the top of her suitcase and closed the lid. She also had been given no choice.

Outside, the sound of a stretcher being wheeled out from Casualty entrance made her move swiftly. Whether she liked it or not, Laura was going to Canberra.

The girl—Barbara—desperately wanted to accompany her boyfriend, and both Laura and Ben thought it wise to let her have her way.

'These cuts could probably do with the attention of a plastic surgeon,' Ben told Laura when both patients were loaded into the vehicle. 'Besides, the boy is going to need all the support he can get if he's going to make it.'

Laura nodded and then made to climb up into the back of the cab after them. As she did, Ben touched her lightly on the shoulder, making her pause.

'Get some rest,' he said firmly. 'When you get back here again you're on your own, and you'll have to be fit.' He turned and walked haltingly back into the hospital.

Laura stared at his retreating figure as the ambulance

started moving out of the hospital grounds. She knew what she was being told: for the time Ben Durell had to work at Calua Bay, Laura was being banished to Canberra. Her return, no doubt, would be the signal for him to retire back to his fortress on Blackwood Ridge.

The memory of his mouth on hers came fleetingly back to her. The feel of him had scared her as Craig Palmer's vicious assault never had. Ben Durell could break down her barriers, and touch the raw pain within.

If he could do that then it was just as well he had the strength for both of them and was sending her away.

The journey across the mountains, tense and uncomfortable, seemed endless. Laura sat on the cramped seat at the injured boy's head and monitored him like a hawk. At every bump the drips had to be checked, and the breathing tube Ben had inserted monitored to make sure it hadn't moved.

The boy was deeply unconscious, and not for the first time Laura worried about the extent of his head injuries. On the other side of the cabin, the girl lay, her eyes never leaving her boyfriend's face.

'Barbara, why don't you try to sleep?' Laura told her quietly. The girl had been given strong pain-killers, and Laura knew that if she could only relax she would drift into much needed sleep.

'I'm scared he'll die if I do,' the girl whispered. She flashed a half-embarrassed glance up at Laura. 'I supppose that seems stupid. . .'

Laura shook her head. 'I'm watching him, though,' she reassured her. 'And I don't need sleep.'

Barbara didn't answer. She lay back silently and

after a while Laura saw that she was crying. Laura handed her a cloth and when it came away there was blood mingled with the tears. The girl looked at it with dismay and then turned her face away from Laura.

'Do you want to tell me what happened?' Laura asked gently. Perhaps if the girl couldn't sleep it would be better for her to talk than to lie there and fret.

For a long while there was silence. Laura didn't press her. She checked and rechecked the boy at her side, and waited.

'We come from Canberra,' the girl whispered finally. 'We—Chris and I—are uni students. We were invited down to stay in Calua Bay with some friends. A week at the beach seemed terrific and we didn't want to miss any of it. We wanted to be there early on Monday and there was a party in Canberra on Sunday night, so we went to that first. . .' Her voice broke off.

Laura didn't need to hear the rest. The couple still had the faint aroma of alcohol about them. That, combined with fatigue, had proved their undoing.

'He. . . If they do a blood test Chris'll lose his licence,' Barbara whispered, and Laura grimaced. It was to be hoped his licence was all Chris stood to lose.

Finally the ambulance slowed at the outskirts of the city, and as the vehicle pulled into the major entrance of the large hospital Laura sighed with relief. She had done the best she could. Chris was still alive. From here on a skilled team of specialists used to coping with road trauma would take over.

As the doors of the ambulance were flung open Barbara grabbed Laura's hand.

'Thank you,' she faltered. 'Will. . .will I see you again?'

'I'm staying in Canberra until the weekend,' Laura

reassured her. 'I'll come in and see you each day until you leave.' She returned the frightened girl's grasp. 'Good luck,' she said gently.

Then hands reached in to retrieve the two stretchers and Laura was left to officially hand over her patients and leave.

Afterwards she sat in the hospital coffee lounge and considered. Whether she liked it or not she had five days free.

She didn't know Canberra very well. Her training had been Sydney-based. Sydney, with its vast unplanned urban sprawl around its spectacular harbour, seemed friendly and welcoming compared to Australia's capital, Canberra. Here there was no jumble of terraces and crowded shops. Everything was clean and regulated. Laura looked out across bushland to the highway beyond and found difficulty in believing she was in a capital city.

She pulled her purse from her handbag to pay for the coffee and, at the same time, retrieved a folded piece of paper from its depths. Ben had handed it to her at the last minute.

'This is a hotel belonging to friends of mine in the hills above Canberra,' he'd told her. 'It's the perfect place for a good rest.'

Friends of Ben. . . It was as good a reason as any for not going to that hotel, she thought ruefully. The ambulance had passed a big international hotel two blocks from the hospital. Perhaps she could stay there.

There wasn't much rest to be had staying in a huge impersonal hotel, Laura acknowledged honestly. She wouldn't relax, and her battered body demanded rest. Ben had been right to insist she take time off, though it nearly choked her to admit it.

She looked down again at the address on the card. Bellbyre Inn. . . Well, who knew? It could be dreadful. But, if Ben Durell recommended it, the chances of its being dreadful were one in a million.

She crossed the lobby to a bank of pay phones, and dialled the hotel. To her surprise, the man who answered her call knew all about her.

'Dr Haley. Yes, of course we have a vacancy. Ben Durell told us we might expect you. Would you like us to organise transport?'

'No, thank you,' Laura said, more brusquely than intended. After all, the man was only trying to be nice. It wasn't his fault that she felt pushed into things by Ben Durell. 'I'll make my own way out.'

Afterwards she had another cup of coffee before leaving, taking an almost perverse pleasure in her token act of independence. Finally she rose, collected her small suitcase and caught a cab from the rank at the entrance. She cast a doubtful look back at the hospital as she left, her thoughts still on the couple she had accompanied across the mountains. Still, their care was now out of her hands, Dr Laura Haley was now officially on holiday.

As Laura had expected, Ben Durell had not been mistaken when he recommended the Bellbyre Inn.

Laura sat in the taxi, unnoticing, as it drove through the city, her tired mind too exhausted to take more than a cursory interest in the wide tree-lined streets of Australia's capital city. Finally the streets petered out and the suburbs became bushland.

'Lovely spot for a holiday,' the cabbie remarked as he manoeuvred the cab up a steep incline at the end of a gravel road. He swung the taxi into a small gravelled driveway. 'Here you are, lady, and half your luck.'

Laura could only agree. The hotel was a series of low mud-brick apartments, clustered round a vast swimming-pool that seemed to be hewn from natural rock. When Laura investigated further she found that the effect was the result of clever landscaping, a pool with huge boulders set into the side and old tree trunks placed to make natural diving-boards. The still green waters made Laura ache for a swim.

The proprietors were a friendly couple in their forties who greeted Laura with warmth and ill-concealed curiosity. They were friends, Ben had said. It made Laura wonder what he had told them about her. Still, as they sensed her reluctance to talk they abandoned their questions. Laura was shown to a lovely, sunlit apartment overlooking the pool and left to herself.

Her overwhelming sensation as she closed the door behind them was guilt. What on earth was she doing here? Back at Calua Bay, Ben was driving himself to the limit, doing her work, and at Central Hospital Chris was fighting for his life, yet here she was with nothing to do. Nothing to do. . . The phrase echoed over and over in her head and she felt like pinching herself to see if she was dreaming. There was nothing to do until the weekend. Laura's holidays had been taken up by the needs of her mother for so long that the sensation was pure novelty.

The pretty blue and white coverlet on the bed looked soft and inviting. Laura stared down at it and then glanced at her watch. It was four-thirty. She should unpack before dinner. . .

The coverlet was too inviting. Laura sank down on to the soft pillows and, within moments, was asleep.

She was woken by the insistent, jarring ring of the phone. For a moment Laura sat up, confused, unable to remember where she was. Then, as the ringing went on, she located the phone in the deepening dusk and lifted the receiver.

'Laura?'

For a moment Laura stared down at the receiver in shock. Ben. . . Finally she placed the receiver against her ear again, in the manner of one doing something against her better judgement.

'Yes?'

'Don't sound so suspicious. I'm not about to disturb your holiday.'

Laura bit her lip. 'I didn't mean. . .'

He wasn't listening. 'I've rung the hospital and checked on Chris.' His voice was curt. 'I gather it's touch and go. Will you keep me informed?'

'Of course I will.' Laura's voice still sounded defensive, but there was no need. She had intended checking until he was out of danger. She frowned to herself, though. Surely it wasn't part of Ben's job to keep tabs on patients no longer in his care? Unless. . .unless they meant something to him. . .

'Of course I will,' Laura repeated, this time with some warmth in her voice. 'I was going to anyway.'

'I thought you would.' There was a long silence at the end of the phone as if Ben was considering what else to say. He obviously rejected any thoughts that came to mind. 'Enjoy yourself,' he said curtly and hung up. Laura was left staring again at the receiver, a frown puckering her face.

Why was he so concerned? And then she thought back to the events of the day. Ben at the scene of the accident—Ben spending time trying to keep alive a boy trapped in a crumpled car. And Ben Durell hadn't practised medicine since the accident that had claimed the life of his wife.

Laura stirred uneasily, guilt once more nagging at her. She should have insisted on going to the crash scene that morning herself. To force Ben to come face to face with his memories was nothing less than cruel.

It was done now, though. She couldn't undo what had happened, so both she and Ben Durell would be forced to live with it.

Laura spent most of the next couple of days in the hotel. Apart from a daily trip down to the hospital, she had no desire to do anything else. Attached to Reception was a tiny restaurant for patrons only, and Laura's hosts prided themselves on their cuisine. There were few guests.

'At this time of the year most people are at the beach,' Peter, Laura's host, told her.

'More fool them,' Laura smiled. She finished the last of her strawberry crêpe with regret. 'This is heaven.'

'We try to make it like that.' Peter took her empty plate and hesitated before taking it to the kitchen. He and Marie, his French wife, had quickly warmed to the girl their friend had recommended to them. 'You'll be going back to Calua Bay on Saturday?'

'Yes.' Laura took a sip of the excellent coffee and stared down at the damask tablecloth. The bruises on her body had ceased aching, and this time of peace was all too short. She glanced up at Peter. 'How do you know Ben?' she asked curiously.

'Marie was a ballet dancer with Claire,' Peter said, as if that explained everything. And then, at Laura's look of incomprehension, he smiled.

'I'm sorry. I forgot you wouldn't know of Ben's wife, Claire. She danced with the Australian Ballet before she had Zia.'

'Zia?'

'Her daughter.' Peter shrugged. 'Before she married Ben, Claire was married to one of the leading males in the ballet company. Then she had Zia and it broke up the marriage.'

'Why?' Laura had no business asking but she couldn't stop to save herself.

Peter glanced around the near-empty restaurant, mentally checking tables. Those diners remaining were sitting lazily, enjoying a last coffee. There was nothing that needed doing for the moment. With an air of a man about to enjoy himself, Peter pulled out the chair opposite Laura and sat down.

'She couldn't cope,' he confided. 'After the baby she couldn't get her form back to what it was.' He sighed. 'She was perfection to watch. But afterwards. . . Well, it wasn't the same. And her husband. . . He didn't want to know about it. He married her because she was perfect, and he drove her to the limit trying to get back to where she was before pregnancy.'

'Poor girl,' Laura said quietly.

Peter shrugged. 'It was hard, but other dancers have gone through the transition. Take Marie,' he said with simple pride. 'She was a wonderful dancer and then married me, retired and became Australia's best cook. And she's happy.' He hesitated. 'Claire's problem was that her husband didn't think she was great under any other terms than dancing.'

'So they divorced?' Laura interjected.

'Yes. Then she met and married Ben, and the real problems began.'

Laura frowned. 'Why?'

'She didn't exactly come into the marriage unscarred,' Peter said bluntly. 'She saw marriage to Ben as an escape and it was doomed to failure from the start.' He grimaced. 'She had this thing about physical perfection that drove her absolutely. Ben couldn't rid her of the feeling of failure. When she was killed she was down to little over six stone with anorexia nervosa.'

Anorexia nervosa. . . Laura frowned. It was the process of dieting to death, more commonly found among intense teenagers than married women with a child.

'She refused point-blank to have more children too,' Peter said reflectively. 'It hurt Ben very much. He gave the marriage his damnedest, but she was impossible.'

'Why on earth did he marry her?'

Peter smiled. 'If you could have met her you would have understood,' he said slowly. 'Claire was an enchanting, elf-like creature who could twist men around her little finger.'

From the other side of the room a customer raised his hand for service, and Peter rose.

'Duty calls.' He hesitated, looking down at Laura's disturbed face. 'I shouldn't have told you all that,' he said gently. 'But Ben sounded concerned about you when he rang. And Ben hasn't sounded concerned about anyone for a very long time.'

He left her then, and Laura was left to stare into the dregs of her coffee-cup, looking for answers to questions she didn't really understand.

CHAPTER SEVEN

ON TUESDAY the news from the hospital was discouraging, but on Wednesday Chris regained consciousness for a few moments. On impulse Laura bought flowers from the florist near the hospital and made her visit more formal. She had liked what she had seen of Barbara and was becoming increasingly concerned as to what lay in store for the girl. She found her sitting up in bed, surrounded by posies and get-well cards.

Barbara greeted Laura with delight, and accepted the flowers Laura had bought with real pleasure.

'You didn't have to do this.' She buried her nose in the posy. 'Mmm. Isn't the smell just gorgeous? That's crowea augustifolia,' she said, pointing to a spray of white foliage. 'And this here's dentata with the baeckea. And don't the hookerana look superb? They go beautifully with the anigozanthos.'

Laura looked suspiciously down at the flowers and then at the girl admiring them. 'Are you sure you're OK, Barbara?' she asked. 'You look OK but you don't sound it. The florist said this was kangaroo paw, banksia and native backing.'

Barbara laughed. 'Same thing,' she assured Laura. 'I'm a botany student and my area of expertise is Australian flowering plants.' She looked around the room. 'Not that you can tell from the offerings of my friends. Chrysanthemums and gladioli, for heaven's sake!' She looked affectionately down at Laura's posy. 'This is much nicer.'

'You're obviously feeling better, then,' Laura smiled.

'I am.' Barbara hesitated and then met Laura with a direct look. 'It looks as if Chris might be able to stand trial for drink-driving too.'

'I hope so,' Laura said simply. She smiled. 'Not about the drink-driving charge, I guess, but I'd be glad to see him fit enough to face it.' She frowned. 'It's early days yet, though, Barbara. He might have regained consciousness, but his internal injuries are horrific.'

Barbara smiled with the optimism of the young. 'He will,' she said definitely. 'You wait and see.' She hesitated and then forced herself to continue. 'You know, it was so easy,' she said slowly. 'One minute we were happy and sleepy and slightly drunk, and the next we could have been dead. We damn near were.' She grimaced and looked shyly up at Laura. 'I guess you've heard that before,' she said quietly.

Laura shook her head. 'Not as often as I'd like,' she admitted. 'Mostly the people it happens to don't get the opportunity to learn from their mistakes.'

'Well, we've learned.' Barbara fiddled idly with the stem of her posy. 'If Chris recovers. . . When Chris recovers he looks like missing a year of study. A year! One lousy drink too many. . .' She grimaced and then met Laura's look. 'One thing I've decided, though. Chris wanted us to get married at Christmas. I was all for putting it off. Now. . . If he's well we'll be married. Life's too short to put things off,' she added seriously. 'I hadn't realised it until now. But if he loves me. . .'

She looked up at Laura and her fragile optimism shattered. 'Oh, Dr Haley, he will make it, won't he?'

'It's still too soon to tell,' Laura said softly. To tell

the girl anything different would be cruel, especially as
Laura had seen the medical reports and knew what
Chris had to fight.

Barbara stared up at her for a long moment and then
carefully laid the posy on the tray over her bed. 'You
don't believe. . .' Her voice broke on a sob and she
buried her face in her hands.

Chris died late on Thursday night. Laura came into the
hospital when he sank into a coma, and it was she who
broke the news to Barbara, and to Chris's parents. The
hospital doctors treated Laura as if she were the boy's
general practitioner, and, as he didn't seem to have
such a thing, she reluctantly accepted her role.

When there was nothing left for her to do she caught
a taxi back out to Bellbyre, feeling tired and dispirited.
It all seemed such a waste.

The hotel was in darkness when she arrived. Laura
glanced at her watch. The luminous dial said one-
thirty. The little hotel was sleepy at the best of times
and the patrons had obviously long since gone to bed.

She made her way to her room overlooking the pool
and slowly prepared for bed. The tragedy was still with
her, hanging on her heart with dreary reality. Back at
the hospital, Barbara had been sedated to pass the
night, but she knew the girl had more than one night
to pass. She had the rest of her life to face without the
man she loved.

When would she get used to it? Laura wondered
drearily. After four years of practising medicine she
should be inured to tragedy. Perhaps she never could
be.

She slipped under the cool sheets, stared at the
flickering moonlight on the ceiling and waited for sleep.

An hour later sleep was no closer. In desperation she turned on her light and rose to put on the jug for a cup of tea. As the jug reached boiling, the telephone at her bedside started to ring.

Laura knew without answering it who it would be. She turned off the jug and went to sit on the bed before lifting the receiver.

'Ben?' she said softly.

'You told me you'd let me know.' His voice was flat and emotionless.

'I was going to contact you in the morning. I thought it would be too late when I got back to the hotel.'

'You've been out?' It was an accusation, and the words made Laura pause before she responded.

'I've been at the hospital since early evening,' she said quietly. 'Barbara wanted me. She hasn't any parents and needed someone. . .' She took a deep breath. 'Is that OK with you, Dr Durell?'

There was long silence. When Ben spoke again his voice had changed. 'His death was inevitable,' he said. 'I knew that on Monday.' He paused again. 'I knew it before we cut him from the damned car.'

'You had to try, though,' Laura said gently. 'That's what our job is.'

He didn't hear her. And in a moment Laura wished him goodnight and replaced the receiver.

She slept late the next morning, woke to croissants and coffee in bed, then slipped into a bikini and took a book out to the pool. The hotel boasted an excellent library of whodunits, a selection that exactly suited Laura's present inclination.

The tragedy of the night before was still with her, but she had seen enough deaths in Casualty over the years to have learned to put it to the back of her mind.

She rang the hospital mid-morning and spoke briefly to Barbara, but this morning an aunt had materialised and was taking the girl home. With relief Laura realised that her responsibility had ended.

She lay under the shade of the eucalypts, with the sunlight filtering through the canopy of leaves to warm her as she read. Canberra was sweltering in summer heat, but for Laura it was no problem. As she became too warm for comfort she slid her body into the crystal-clear pool, then emerged to sleep or read again.

Marie brought salads out to the pool-side at lunch-time, and she and Peter joined her for lunch. Then they left her to it. Laura slept, swam, and slept again.

At dusk she stirred reluctantly from her favourite lounger by the pool. As she gathered her towels together Peter came to find her.

'Ben rang,' he said. 'He's coming down.'

'Ben!' Laura stared at Peter blankly. 'Did he say why?'

Peter shook his head. 'He'll be here by eight-thirty, he reckons, and he wondered if you'd wait and have dinner with him.'

Laura looked at Peter for an unbelieving moment and then shook her head. 'He didn't say that,' she said definitely. 'At a guess, it was something like, "I'll be there by eight-thirty. Don't give Dr Haley anything to eat until then."'

Peter grinned. 'You do know our Ben,' he chuckled. 'Will you wait?'

Laura hesitated. To refuse would appear churlish, to Peter as well as Ben. 'OK,' she agreed.

Peter smiled and then hesitated. 'How would it be if Marie and I joined you?' he asked. 'We've an appren-tice who wants to have a go at cooking without supervision, and we're both ready for a night off. If it's OK with you, we'll get dressed up and have a night off in style.'

Somewhat to her surprise, Laura found herself looking forward to dinner. The pleasures of eating in solitary state had begun to pall. She had to admit too that there was a part of her that very much wanted to see Ben Durell again.

Why was he coming? Was it something to do with the previous night? Or had the responsibility of Calua Bay's medical needs become too much?

She grimaced. After tomorrow those medical needs would be back firmly on her shoulders, and she was becoming increasingly unsure as to whether her shoulders were broad enough to take the strain.

Still, tonight she was free, and Ben was coming.

Ben. . . His image had crept into her mind over and over during the past week. She had pushed it aside, annoyed with herself, but the image persisted.

After tomorrow she could well not see him again, she knew. Once she was back working as Calua Bay's general practitioner he could retreat to Blackwood Ridge and she would be left alone.

Laura flicked open her suitcase and stared into its depths. 'We'll get dressed up,' Peter had said. There was nothing suitable for a formal dinner here. As she pondered Marie knocked and entered.

'Clean towels,' she smiled, laying a pile of white towels down on the bed. She glanced across at Laura and the open suitcase. 'Problems?'

Laura shook her head, but Marie was already walking over to the case. She lifted one dress up, shook her head, then another and then the last.

'I see,' she said slowly. 'None of these is right. They're all day dresses.'

'They'll have to do,' Laura said shortly. 'It doesn't matter.'

Marie looked thoughtfully at her. 'I think it does. I tell you,' she smiled, her French accent more pronounced as she became thoughtful, 'if Ben Durell were taking me to dinner I would not wear these.'

'They're all I've got,' Laura said helplessly. 'I didn't count on a formal dinner when I packed. Besides, Ben Durell isn't taking me to dinner. I'm having dinner with you and Peter, and Ben's just one of four.'

Laura was ignored. Marie was standing back, looking at Laura's slim form consideringly. 'We're the same size,' she announced with satisfaction. 'And I have the very thing.'

Two minutes later she was back. Draped over her arm was a skirt and blouse in a creamy peach silk. The blouse had half-sleeves, but there any hint of modesty ended. The neckline plunged straight down, front and back, and a tiny thread of cream beading edged its boundary. The skirt was wide-waisted and flared out to mid-calf. Laura looked at it in dismay.

'I can't wear that, Marie,' she said firmly. 'What if I spilt something?'

'The outfit is made to be worn.' Marie was pulling Laura's sandals out and holding them against the clothes. 'With my opportunities for night-life here, it will never be worn out. And these will do,' she said triumphantly. The sandals were high, strappy cream leather. They blended in beautifully with the silk. 'Now. . . The hair. . .'

'My hair is fine,' Laura said defensively. Since she

had just come out of the pool, it wasn't fine at all, but a shower and shampoo would fix that.

'Must you still wear the bandage?' Marie demanded.

'I. . . No. . . I guess it could come off now,' Laura admitted.

'Good. If you let your curls wave around your face you will not look injured.'

'I hardly think Ben's likely to worry about whether I have a scar,' Laura said tightly, and Marie shrugged.

'Who knows?' she said expressively. 'He cannot seem to forget his own.'

Laura bit her lip. Here it was again, the fear of repugnance that Ben walked with. Why? she wondered, when he was so damned attractive? She turned back to the clothes lying on the bed.

'I can't wear these,' she said again.

Marie looked at Laura for a long moment, and Laura was left with the uncomfortable feeling that the French woman saw more than she wanted her to know.

'It would give me pleasure if you wore them,' she said simply. 'Ben Durell is our very dear friend.'

'That's got nothing to do with me borrowing your clothes,' Laura protested. Marie smiled.

'*Au contraire*,' she said quietly. 'It has everything to do with it.' She smiled gently at Laura and walked out of the room.

An hour later Laura was as ready as she ever would be. She flicked the brush through her shoulder-length curls and gazed dispassionately into the mirror. The reflection that met her eyes was not her own.

The outfit was right for her. On Marie's dark colouring it would have looked great, but for Laura it was perfection. The soft peach colour made her creamy white skin look almost translucent. The silk clung alluringly to her body and the neckline swept down to reveal the soft rounded swell of her breasts.

Laura had washed her hair and let it dry without combing it away from her face. It wisped and flamed around her cheeks, framing the huge green eyes. Her make-up was simple. With such clothes anything else would appear heavy. The bruises and cut on the side of her face had all but disappeared under the curls. She looked unmarked.

'I look like a Dresden doll,' she said disparagingly in to the mirror, but Marie, coming quietly into the room to see how she was progressing, disagreed with vigour.

'A Dresden doll. . . Not one bit,' she laughed. 'When would a man ever want to make love to a Dresden doll? And if Ben Durell doesn't want to make love to you in that outfit he is not human.'

Laura turned worried eyes to the Frenchwoman. 'I don't want him to make love to me,' she said quietly.

'Now that. . .' Marie said with finality as she flicked an expert finger through the folds of Laura's skirt, 'is one big lie. Me, I know. I see it in your eyes. There is a hunger there. . .'

'There is not,' Laura said desperately. 'I don't need a man. . .'

Marie stood back and looked at her. 'Maybe not,' she agreed at last. 'Maybe not any man. Maybe you only have need for our Dr Durell.' She cast a last critical look over Laura. 'Now come,' she said firmly. 'He is here.'

Laura started. 'Here! Already. . .'

Marie smiled. 'He arrived fifteen minutes ago and has changed already. I left him drinking beer in the kitchen with Peter. Now you are here, we proceed to the dining-room and drink champagne. Yes?' There was nothing more to be said.

It was absurd to feel this shy. Laura entered the big kitchen, feeling about fifteen years old.

No fifteen-year-old would get the reception accorded her, however. Peter stood with alacrity and let his breath out in a long whistle of appreciation.

'Wow!'

Laura smiled, yet her eyes were on Ben. He didn't say anything but she had his attention. His eyes raked her body and his mouth seemed to tighten. Laura shrugged inwardly, disappointed. So much for the effect she had on him.

The effect he had on her was impossible to ignore, however. He wore a black dinner jacket and stark white dress shirt, and she had never seen a man more attractive. The scar added to his attractiveness. His deep-tanned face with its chiselled bone-structure and harsh scarring was a face that seemed as if it was burning into her soul. It almost made her want to weep.

'Ben,' she said quietly in greeting.

'Dr Haley.' His tone was equally formal. Beside Ben, Peter raised his eyebrows to the heavens.

'Now there's a great way to welcome such beauty,' he chided his friend. 'Dr Haley, indeed! Even I only called her Dr Haley once.'

His wife rapped him playfully on the arm. 'That is because you are the greatest flirt in Canberra,' she said firmly.

'And the luckiest man,' Peter agreed with ease. He swung his wife against him and squeezed her to his body. 'I've Australia's most beautiful woman, my

closest friend and the second loveliest woman as well
to take to dinner.'

Marie eyed him with suspicion. 'Which is which?'
she demanded.

'I refuse to answer on the grounds that I'm preju-
diced,' Peter answered with aplomb. He gave her
another squeeze of pure affection and they laughed.

Even Ben's austerity was not proof against his hosts'
easy charm. Before entrée, Marie and Peter had them
in a ripple of laughter, which didn't let up until coffee
was served. Then Marie broke the magic.

'Will you be seeing Zia before you return
tomorrow?' she asked Ben.

The smile faded from Ben's eyes. 'If she'll see me,'
he said shortly.

'If she'll see you?' Marie gasped. 'What sort of silly
nonsense is this? Who pays her school fees, Ben
Durell?'

'It doesn't mean she has to see me,' Ben said harshly.
'There's no compulsion.'

Marie glared across the table, and Laura knew that
the glare was intended for the absent Zia. 'She's old
enough to accept responsibility for her own actions,
Ben. She should be told how hurtful her behaviour is.'

Ben shrugged. 'It would change nothing,' Ben said
slowly. 'At least she's honest.'

Peter moved in then, adroitly changing the topic
from one that had upset his wife and caused the set,
bitter look to descend on his friend's face.

'Take Laura with you when you go to Zia's school
tomorrow,' he suggested. 'I'll bet she hasn't seen how
the upper crust educate their kids these days. Honestly. . .' he turned to Laura '. . .the kids in Zia's
school have a computer prescribed as a prerequisite.

When the day girls leave the place each night you see the society ladies of tomorrow, climbing into the Mercedes or the Rolls, all clutching their lap-top computers in their elegantly gloved little hands.'

'There speaks a state-school kid if ever I heard one,' Marie laughed. 'It's my belief that you're jealous, Peter.'

'Jealous! Me? You've got to be joking. Show me the computer that can outcalculate me and I'll eat my Sunday dinner. . .'

Amid laughter the conversation moved to more general topics.

Laura was silent for the majority of the meal, content to let the talk and laughter wash around her. Marie and Peter were nice, she decided, and they certainly brought out a side of Ben she had never seen before. The tight, strained look around his eyes relaxed, and he shed years with it.

He glanced down at one stage and caught her eyes on him. Furious with herself, Laura flushed and turned back to where Marie was holding forth on the delights of French cooking.

'Speaking of which, I must get back to it,' she said contritely as she finished her second cup of coffee. She screwed up her little nose. 'I have beef on the menu tomorrow night and the marinade has to be prepared before bed tonight.'

'I'll help you,' Peter said quickly, standing as well. He smiled down at the two still seated. 'If I were you I'd take Laura up to the look-out,' he told Ben. 'It's her last night here, and a girl shouldn't miss out on a sight like that.'

'Thank you, Peter,' Ben said drily. 'I don't believe my leg would take me that far.'

'You never know till you try,' Peter said with a twinkle. 'Go on, Ben. Be a devil.' He turned and walked swiftly away before Ben could retaliate.

As they left, Laura also rose. 'I. . . I think I'd better be going too,' she said softly.

'Why?' Ben's black eyes were watching hers with a look she didn't really understand.

'I'm tired. . . We've a long day ahead of us tomorrow. . .'

'You've had a week's holiday,' Ben said firmly, standing as well and reaching for the cane left propped against the table. 'If I'm not tired you can't be. Come on, then.' His voice was goaded.

'Wh. . .where?'

'To the look-out, of course. Didn't you know that Ben Durell always does what he's told?'

Laura shook her head, her eyes containing a trace of laughter. 'No,' she said solemnly.

'Well, I do.' His eyes glinted, dark and dangerous. 'Especially when it's in my best interests.'

They didn't talk again until they were several hundred yards from the hotel. A meandering path wound its way through the thick bushland. On a moonless night the walk would be impossible, Laura thought, but tonight the moon was a great golden ball, lighting the sky and the path before them. Laura's high heels made her careful, although perhaps not as much as her fierce concentration of the ground suggested.

'Have Marie and Ben looked after you?'

'Yes. Thank you.' Laura was silent for a moment and then forced herself to continue. 'They're a lovely couple. I gather they're good friends.'

'As close as any,' he said brusquely, and Laura felt she had been rebuffed.

'Look, you don't have to come on this walk,' she snapped. 'It wasn't my idea.'

'Nor mine either, I seem to remember. However, having come this far, I'm damned if I'm turning back now.'

'So you can prove that you've done it,' Laura said bitterly.

'Yes.' His tone was harsh. 'I'm doing all I can to get this leg working again. I thought that was what you wanted.'

'I couldn't care less what you do with your rotten leg,' Laura flung at him. 'If I were your treating doctor I'd be telling you to get some decent physiotheraphy. But I'm not. As an indifferent bystander, I can tell you it would give me profound satisfaction if it dropped off.'

'Now, how could an indifferent bystander possibly want my leg to drop off?' Ben mused, and there was laughter in his voice.

'He would if he knew you,' Laura snapped. She stalked on ahead, but the dignity of her move was marred by a root, sticking treacherously a quarter of an inch above the surface of the path. She stumbled and would have fallen, but Ben was too fast. As her arm fell foward to try to save herself it was caught in a grip of iron and she was steadied.

'I. . . Thank you.' Laura fought for words, temporarily shocked out of anger. She pulled her arm back but the grip tightened.

'You know, if we are forced to continue with this walk, we may as well enjoy it,' Ben said.

Laura wrenched her arm away. 'I'm enjoying it,' she said bitterly. 'I'm having a wonderful time. Any fool can see Dr Laura Haley is having the time of her life.'

There was a long silence again. Finally Laura broke it. 'You shouldn't be here,' she said crossly. 'You promised you'd look after the practice. How could you leave with patients in hospital?'

'You think I'm negligent?' he said quietly.

'What else can I think?' Laura's face was crimson from tension.

He stopped and took her shoulder, swinging her roughly around to face him. 'I'm no Cliff Paige,' he said harshly. 'That place is impossible to run effectively as a one-doctor practice. It's just too damned far to get help. Paige used to just walk out whenever he wanted a weekend off.'

'And isn't that what you've done?' she said, wanting, for some obscure reason, to hurt him.

'No, it's not.' He let her go again and started walking. Laura watched him go for a moment, then shrugged and kept on. 'A friend dropped in to see me this morning, meaning to stay for the weekend. Fortunately for us he happens to be an old medical colleague.' In the dark Laura couldn't see Ben's face, but she heard the smile in his voice. 'He went to Blackwood Ridge and Joe told him where to find me. He came down to the clinic to see for himself, and before he knew it he had a job for the weekend.'

'You just left him. . .?'

'I just left him.' Ben looked back to where Laura was struggling with her high-heeled shoes, sighed and took her arm again, tightening his grip as he felt her resistance. 'It'll do him good,' he assured her. 'Rod's a radiologist. It'll be good for his medicine to remember what the real world is like.'

'Oh, Ben. . .' Laura was half shocked, half laughing. . .

'"Oh, Ben,"' he mocked her. His grip tightened on her arm. 'What happened between you and Ross?' he asked suddenly.

Laura gasped with the sheer shock of the question. 'I don't. . . What business is it of yours?'

'None,' he admitted. 'I simply wanted to know.'

Laura fell silent for a moment. They kept walking, Ben seemingly content to wait for her to form an answer to his question.

'We broke off our engagement,' she said finally.

'Who broke it off? Ross or you?'

Laura glared up at him, but Ben was watching the path ahead. His expression was one of indifference. And all of a sudden it was easier to talk than to stay silent.

'I broke it off,' Laura said slowly. 'I hardly had a choice when I discvoered he was sharing his bed with another woman.'

Ben's eyebrows were raised but he said nothing. Laura stumbled again and his hand steadied her.

'Was that a shock?' he asked.

'What do you think?' Laura was silent for a long moment, her thoughts drifting back to that last dreadful scene. And yet she should have known. . . She should have expected it.

'Ross is a doctor too,' Laura continued and her tone was that of someone almost speaking to herself. 'We went through uni together, and always assumed we would be married. But my mother—well, after Dad died she just sort of shrivelled, and by the time I graduated she couldn't be left alone.'

'So?' Ben's voice came from a long way away and hardly interrupted her thoughts.

'I was still living at home. Mum was weak and

disorientated, but while she stayed at home she seemed happy enough. I hired a nurse to be with her while I was at work.'

Ben whistled. 'That must have cost a fortune.'

'It was worth it,' Laura said fiercely. 'There was no money at all after Dad got sick, and Mum did other people's housework to keep me at school. It seemed the least I could do.'

'But Ross didn't see it like that.'

'No,' Laura said grimly. 'He thought I was wasting our money. And then he had the offer of a practice on the north coast. By that time it was clear that Mum was slowly dying. He wanted me to put her in a nursing home and go with him.'

'And did you?'

'I did for a while,' Laura said sadly. 'I let him talk me into it. Mum was so confused that she didn't seem to know me and Ross—well, he was my future. So I put her in a home and went with him. But a fortnight later I came back to visit and couldn't believe the change.' She looked up at Ben, willing him to understand her logic.

'In a strange place it was as if she was already dead,' Laura said sadly. 'She just lay and stared at the wall and waited to die.' She bit her lip. 'And the nursing staff kept calling her dearie. . .'

'So you took her back home.'

Laura nodded. 'I would have taken her north with me, but Ross wouldn't have a bar of the idea. So I stayed in Sydney, did my anaesthetic first part and waited for Mum to die. And Ross waited for me to come. Or he said he did. After the funeral I was feeling so desolate that I drove through the night to reach Ross earlier than I'd told him.' She shrugged. 'I reached his house at five in the morning and he wasn't alone. End of story.'

'And you took the job at Calua Bay.'

'I wanted out of Sydney and away from anything that reminded me of Mum or Ross. I also love the sea. Calua Bay was the first job on offer, even if it may only be temporary.' She bit her lip. 'I couldn't afford to be choosy. I couldn't bear to stay in the city and I was flat broke. The cost of nursing Mum at home in the end was prohibitive.'

'I see.' Ben was silent for a moment. Ahead of them the path opened out to a plateau. 'Hence your interest in nursing homes.'

'I did the rounds when I was looking for somewhere for Mum,' Laura agreed. 'I got to know what made a good one.'

'And Sunset Lodge doesn't come up to scratch.'

'Not by a long shot.'

They had come to the path's end. Where they came to a halt was a single steel rail between them and a sheer drop down into the valley.

The view was staggering. Below them, the lights of Canberra glimmered and winked in the night, sprawling out over the plain. From where they stood they could see clearly the surging arc of water from the fountain on Lake Burley Griffin, floodlit in spectacular glory. Above the town, a myriad stars and a golden moon hung in the black of the night sky.

It was almost too beautiful to bear. Laura felt tears well in her eyes. The beauty before her, the man at her side and the memories she had just allowed to come to her overwhelmed her with emotion. She stood, her hands clasping the cool steel of the handrail, and waited for something she didn't understand.

'Do you still love him?'

Laura stared down at the city below them and her mind slowly cleared. And suddenly the truth was crystal-clear.

'No,' she said honestly. She ventured a look up at the man beside her and then away. 'He still wanted to marry me, you know,' she said conversationally. 'He said it was a one-night stand and I was silly to take it seriously. For a while I regretted my pride, which wouldn't let me go back to him. But not now. . . Not any more. . .' She smiled suddenly and the stars brightened, the strange oppression lifting. 'I'm better off on my own.'

'On your own?'

'Yes,' she said definitely, almost defiantly. 'On my own. My medicine's all I need now.'

There was a long silence. Laura's feet were hurting in her unsuitable shoes and she slipped them off, unobtrusively wiggling her toes on the rocks.

'It will improve now.'

Ben's voice when he finally spoke sounded as if he was making a huge effort, and Laura dragged her thoughts to attention to hear what he had just said.

'Wh. . .what will improve?' She turned slightly to him and looked up. Suddenly the move was a mistake. The lightness she had been feeling dissipated and dissolved around her and she was left breathless. The harshness of Ben's features met her eyes. His dark, sardonic gaze filled her vision and she felt herself tremble.

'Sunset Lodge.' Ben was staring down at her as though he was trapped. 'There are already changes being made. . .'

'What sort of changes?' Laura was staring, trying to

adjust to the conversation shift. Ben sounded for all the world like a man trying to distract himself.

Ben didn't answer. It seemed as if he couldn't. For a long moment he closed his eyes, as if he was in unbearable pain. Then he opened them and swore softly.

'Hell!'

'What's wrong?' Laura's eyes didn't leave his face. She was like a rabbit caught in bright headlights, frightened almost to death but unable to move to save herself.

Ben's hands reached up and grasped Laura's shoulders. As his fingers touched the sheer silk fabric of her sleeves Laura felt him flinch. His grip tightened, though. And then his mouth came down to meet hers.

It was a kiss to end all kisses. It was a kiss of longing, desire and heartbreak. It was a kiss of two bodies belonging together, whether or not the minds of each acknowledged it.

Around them the night was a blur of gentle warmth and starlit sky, and Laura's body responded with a burgeoning song of joy. Here was her place. She had just said that medicine was all she would ever need. It was a barefaced lie. This was where she wanted to be. This was all in life that could ever matter.

Her hands came up and held Ben's face to her, deepening the kiss. Beneath her fingers she felt the scar on the side of his face, and her fingers very slowly started to trace its course.

He knew what she was doing. She felt his body stiffen, but she knew that she must continue. The scars on his face stood between Ben and the rest of the world. They couldn't be allowed to be between them.

His tongue was still as she traced the outlines of the

old wound on his face, and his body was motionless.
Laura's fingers were feather-light; hardly touching and
yet wanting to know every trace of him. She felt the
smooth surface of the skin graft and its roughened
edges. And, as her fingers traced their course, her own
tongue came out and started an exploration of its own.

The slow exploration of his face over, her fingers
came away and down to touch his hands. The coarser
surface of his hands was cool to her touch. Still he did
not move. Her fingers twined into his, and her body
was doing its own pleading. Forget the scars, her body
was saying. There are no scars for me. There is nothing
for me except you. And I want you. . . I want you. . .

And suddenly she knew that she was heard. Suddenly there was nothing between them; no yesterday
inflicting its pain and heartbreak. And Laura's pleading
could cease. There was no need. In fact, if she pleaded
to be left alone now she doubted she could make
herself heard.

His hands were pulling her body to his, feeling the
soft, smooth contours of her breasts through the sheer
silk, slipping down to grasp her slender waist and then
holding her thighs in against the hard, unyielding
masculinity of his body. His mouth enveloped hers,
and his tongue possessed her utterly.

There was nothing, nobody else in the world between
them. Laura's head swam in a delirium of joy. Her
hands tugged his body against hers, her small fingers
gripping under his arms, holding her to him. He was so
large. . .he was so male. . .

The sound of laughter brought them apart. From
below them, where the track melted into the dark
canopy of trees, the sounds of people approaching
broke their spell. As they turned, still loosely linked,

they saw more guests from the hotel emerging on to the plateau.

Laura made to draw away, but Ben's hands still held her. 'Afraid of public scrutiny, little one?' he teased her, and Laura gazed up at him in wonder.

'That, coming from you?' she whispered.

He smiled, and his smile was of a man who could conquer the world. His arms dropped and he clasped her hands. 'Come on,' he told her. 'Let's get you home.' He looked down at her bare feet and grinned. 'And you get yourself decent. I refuse to be seen cavorting with naked nymphs at midnight.' He gave her seconds to slide her feet back into her shoes, then led the way home, his limp almost imperceptible as he strode along the bushland path.

They didn't talk on the way down, but it was a different silence than before. Each seemed almost afraid to speak, afraid to break the spell of enchantment over them. In every break of the trees the silver moonlight shone on their faces, deepening the sense of enchantment.

Then they were back at the hotel. As the path brought them out into the courtyard around the pool Laura hesitated, but the hand leading her on was inexorable.

'Don't stop now, my lovely.' Ben's voice was full of love and laughter. 'Or. . .' He hesitated and swung her around, pulling her body into his. 'Are you suddenly feeling shy?'

Laura put a finger up and touched his lips. 'N. . . no,' she whispered. 'Not shy. . .'

'What, then?' His hand cupped her chin, pulling her gaze up to meet hers. And then, at the look of

uncertainty in her eyes, he smiled, and his smile made
Laura's heart turn over within.

'I won't hurt you,' he promised. He bent and kissed
her tenderly on the mouth. 'I'll never hurt you.'

The tenderness and the longing in his voice made
any threads of lingering doubt in Laura's mind dissolve
and float away into the night sky. She lifted her arms
to wind them about his head, but felt instead his arms
seize and lift her against him. The cane was forgotten.
It lay abandoned on the leaf-strewn lawn until the
gardener picked it up and placed it to one side the
following morning.

Laura could never afterwards remember how they
took those last few steps. Somehow they were at the
door of Ben's room and the door was opening inwards.
And somehow she was on the vast bed lit by a shaft of
moonlight in the centre of the room.

Her body was ablaze with wanting, so much that she
almost cried out with frustration as he made her wait.

'We must, my love,' he told her as he left her for a
moment. 'Unless you're into nappies and three a.m.
feeds. . .'

A corner of Laura's mind registered that Ben had
wanted this to happen, had come prepared for such an
eventuality. Her heart did nothing but rejoice in the
knowledge.

Then he was back with her. The flimsy fabric was
lifted away from her skin. Her bra was next, falling
swiftly against the urgency of his fingers. Then there
was only the tiny wisp of her panties, and she was
naked for him. She was his.

His eyes devoured her in the moonlight. He drank
in the smooth, flawless beauty of her. He didn't touch

her. She stood, exposed in the rays of silver, glorying in her nakedness; wanting him to savour her.

He put his hand up and smoothed the hair from her face, exposing for the first time the skilfully stitched wound at her hairline.

'I'll take the stitches out tomorrow,' he promised. 'Does it still hurt?'

'Only when I laugh,' Laura assured him.

He ran his finger slowly down her face. 'Bastard!' he said quietly. 'I didn't hit him hard enough.'

Laura smiled up at him. 'I hear you fractured his jaw as it is,' she said demurely. 'That'll do nicely, thank you. After all, he has to make do with prison for recuperation, and I've got Bellbyre Inn.' And I've got you, her mind was adding. I've got you. . .

Ben's fingers left her face. Then, as he reached for her body with hands that were almost reverent, she moved her own fingers to dispense with his clothes.

His body was as she had known it would be. It was pure steel, strong and hard and unyielding. His muscles stood out in his lean, strong frame. His nakedness filled the room, and she wanted him.

They stood, breast to breast, their skin a hair's breadth apart and yet not touching. Slowly Laura lifted her hand and ran her fingers down through the coarse dark hairs of his chest. She ran her hand down, down until his eyes widened in shock, and a gasp of pure amazement filled the room.

And then she was lifted, lifted in triumph and cradled against his hard, demanding body and his mouth was on hers. The kiss was not enough. They had to be closer.

The bed received their melting bodies. Laura sank

into the pillows and her arms held her man to her. She
wouldn't let him go. She couldn't.

And then she was his. His body entered hers with
triumphant ecstasy and the moon and the stars collided.
It was a thousand suns exploding around them as the
world became theirs and they became one.

CHAPTER EIGHT

LAURA woke to brilliant sunlight, and a happiness she had never known. It was as if the whole world had lit up from the inside, casting brilliance on places that had only known shadow.

What she had known with Ross was nothing compared to this. Their love-affair had been chaste and mundane, filling a need in Laura for security and companionship but little else. Here, beside this man, she felt as if she had just been born.

She opened her eyes wide and stared into the lightness, feeling Ben's naked skin against hers. Her body was curled into the curve of his body and his arm was possessively holding her, even in sleep. Laura gave a tiny wriggle of sheer animal ecstasy and felt him stir against her.

'Lie still, woman,' he grumbled. 'Night's for sleeping.'

'It's not night,' she told him, moving deliciously in his arms until she had twisted to face him. The feel of his body. . . She put a finger out and touched his shuttered eyelids. 'It's after seven.'

'Still night,' he said definitely. His hands moved to accommodate her new position, and then kept moving. Her skin was silk under his hands. Laura felt the breath go out of her in a little rush as she felt him pulling her closer.

'Do you really want to sleep?' she teased him.

'Well. . .' The word was drawn out and considering.

135

His hands were on her thighs, gently stroking, arousing her to a point where her body was moving of its own accord. 'Can you think of anything better to do?'

'We could have a swim,' Laura said slowly. 'A cold swim might be just what I need.'

'It might be just what I need too,' he smiled. His voice was thick, muffled by her hair. 'You're going to have to do something about this hair,' he told her sternly. 'I can't open my eyes for fear of being blinded.'

'It's awful,' she said contritely. 'I could cut it off or dye it. I've often fancied myself as a blonde.'

Regardless of risk, Ben opened his eyes, his look savouring the tousled red curls of the girl in his arm. His hand came through and lifted a wisping strand, running it through his fingers. 'It'd be bloody sacrilege,' he growled. He curled more into his hands, playing with it, touching her scalp and sending electric currents of heat through her body.

'I like your hair too,' Laura confessed. She touched Ben's jet-black hair with her soft hand. 'Even though it does need a cut.'

He pushed her back from him and frowned. 'A cut?' he said blankly.

'A cut,' she said. 'I hate to be the one to tell you this, but it looks like a dog's breakfast.' She smiled lovingly and relented. 'Well, perhaps not quite a dog's breakfast. But unkempt, just the same.'

'A dog's. . .' He stared. 'You don't mind my scars but you object to my hair?'

Laura took a deep breath. 'Ben, of course I don't mind the scars,' she said gently. 'The scars are you. They're what you are. And I love. . .'

The words suddenly ran out. All of a sudden Laura couldn't go on. Ben was staring at her as if he was seeing a ghost, a ghost of which he no longer wanted any part.

'I'm sorry,' Laura whispered. 'I didn't mean it.' She bent forward and kissed him on the lips. Let him not take me seriously, her mind was pleading. This man wants no long-term commitment. Take this moment, because it's all there is. Don't push him. . .

'Didn't you?' His voice was expressionless.

'I told you,' Laura said softly. 'No matter what I say when I'm making love, I've done with men. All I want is my profession.'

The smile that Laura loved came back, and her heart wrenched within her. Ben's dark eyes filled with wicked laughter and he rose on an elbow to look down at her.

'Do you mean you want me to go away?' he demanded.

Laura put a finger up and touched the coarse, wiry hairs on his muscled chest. 'N. . .not yet,' she whispered. 'Not yet.'

For a long moment Ben said nothing, just stayed looking down at her huge green, wonder-filled eyes. Then, as if he couldn't help himself, his mouth lowered on to hers, and his strong arms took her again to himself. The morning warmth enfolded them and they were lost to everything but each other.

Afterwards Laura drifted into a euphoric sleep. She woke to a gentle tap on the door, and opened her eyes to see Ben sitting upright, swiftly pulling on his trousers. For a moment she lay confused, and then the gentle tapping sounded again. Ben rose, strode over and threw open the door as Laura frantically pulled a sheet up and around her.

It was Peter. He strode in bearing a loaded tray. 'Well, well, well,' he beamed at the two of them. 'If

Marie wasn't right all along.' He grinned down at the blushing Laura, supremely unconcerned by her discomfiture. 'I took a tray to your room quarter of an hour ago and couldn't wake you. When I took the tray back to the kitchen Marie just laughed, made up a tray for two and sent it along here.' He smiled and put the tray down on the table. 'Will there be anything more *madame* and *m'sieur* require of the management?'

'A spot of privacy might be nice,' Ben said threateningly and Peter laughed.

'OK, OK, I can take a hint,' he grinned. 'I've never been a man to come between two star-crossed lovers.' He walked to the door and then looked back. 'And can I venture to suggest Bellbyre Inn as a magnificent venue for wedding receptions?' Then, as Ben took a menacing step towards him, he held up his hands in mock surrender and hastily retreated, closing the door behind him.

Ben moved the tray over to the bedside table and sat down beside Laura, handing her a plate loaded with a fragrant, fresh-baked croissant without a word. Laura cast an anxious look up at Ben's face, but it was shuttered and expressionless.

'He was only joking,' she said softly.

'Yes.' Ben buttered his croissant and bit into it mechanically. Then he looked down at the girl beside him.

'I'm not. . . I don't want marriage,' he told Laura. His mouth tightened. 'God knows you've dragged me out into the outside world with a vengeance, but I'm not about to make another commitment based on. . .'

'Based on a one-night stand,' Laura finished for him. Her croissant tasted like ashes in her mouth but she forced herself to keep eating.

'It wasn't that.' He wouldn't meet her eyes.

'No?' She managed a weak smile and reached to pour herself coffee. 'Why did you come here, Ben?'

He shrugged. 'I don't know,' he confessed. He was silent for a moment. 'That damned kid's death. It threw me—made me relive a lot of memories I'd rather be without. And when he died—I guess I assumed you'd be feeling the same. . .'

'And I'm not?'

'You seem to have recovered extremely quickly.' His voice was bitter.

Laura frowned. 'Ben, it really upset me,' she said quietly. 'But Chris was a patient, and I can't afford to dwell on his death. If I do that I'll go mad. I sure as heck won't be able to practise medicine.'

'And medicine's your life,' he said quietly.

Laura took a mouthful of coffee and then another. Finally she found the courage to look up at him. 'Yes,' she said. 'Medicine's my life.' She threw the sheet away from her and crossed to the privacy of the bathroom.

Laura showered swiftly. Afterwards she emerged to find Ben ready to take her place in the shower. It was as if they were strangers, forced to share a room but willing it to end. While he was showering, Laura draped herself respectably with one of the huge white towels, collected last night's clothes and made a quick dash for her own room.

Here she locked the door behind her and dressed automatically in one of her beloved big dresses. Then she stood in front of the mirror, brushing her unruly curls until they shone like burnished copper. The automatic, mechanical movement soothed her frantic mind and gave her time to think.

What had she done? Ben Durell was the second man

in her life she had allowed to make love to her. When she and Ross had made love it had been carefully planned and done with a sense of commitment. They had intended to marry. There was no commitment between Laura and Ben. Ben gave nothing and promised nothing.

For heaven's sake, get away from here, Laura told herself. Get through today and then. . .

And then what? The rest of her life stretched before her as an empty void. There was nothing. Nothing besides Ben. . .

Two weeks ago you'd never met the man, she reminded herself. Two weeks ago all you wanted was medicine. You still even fancied yourself in love with Ross.

Not any more. The memory of Ross had faded to the point where he no longer had the power to hurt her. Ben had at least given her that.

'So can I pick up the threads again?' she asked herself bleakly. 'Can I go back to being a GP in Calua Bay?'

She shook her head slowly. She had come to Calua Bay in ignorance of what the position entailed, and she couldn't do the job. She accepted that now. Cliff Paige had done the job because he was unconcerned about the community's real needs. The community needed more skills than Laura possessed. Regardless as to Cliff Paige's decision, Laura was going to have to move on.

The thought filled her with desolation. Calua Bay was beautiful and she wanted desperately to be a part of the small seaside community. She wanted to see the transformation of Sunset Lodge. She even wanted to see the outcome of her young receptionist's romance.

She shook her head. The place was no position for

an inexperienced young female general practitioner. If Ben hadn't been there Alice would have died and her baby along with her, and Chris would have not been given every chance to live.

If Ben hadn't been there. . . Perhaps she could persuade him. . .

Laura shook he head even as the thought entered her mind. Even if he agreed, she couldn't work beside him—not feeling the way she did.

She gave her hair a last angry brush and threw the hairbrush down on the bed. Damn the man. She had been fine before she had met him. How dared he overthrow her life so completely?

She threw her clothes into her suitcase and then carefully hung Marie's skirt and blouse ready for her to find when the room was done. She looked at them with regret. They were beautiful. They were clothes for happy endings, Laura thought sadly.

'Thanks for trying,' she whispered, and wasn't sure who she was whispering to, Marie or the silk outfit. Finally she did a fast check to make sure she had left nothing behind, closed the case and gave it a kick for good measure. Her red hair bounced around her face as she did so, and, catching sight of her expression in the mirror, she was forced to grin. Here it was again—temper!

'If you hadn't been furious you would have written Ben Durell a nice polite little note explaining your grievances with regard to Sunset Lodge, he would have set the appropriate legal enquiries in motion, and we would never have met,' she told her reflection.

'And you would have been the poorer for it,' her reflection answered her back. 'Even if he doesn't want you—even if it was only for one night. . .'

She fell silent, staring at the mirror. She placed a finger up and ran it down the fading scar at the side of her face. The remembrance of Ben's touch was still with her. She knew that, if he walked through the door right at this minute, she was his.

She emerged from her room with regret, carefully closing the door behind her. She had needed her stay in this place. Her head was healed again and her bruised body recovered. If only it had done the same for her heart. . .

A couple of guests were idly doing laps in the pool. Laura could see no sign of Ben. She set her small suitcase beside a pool-side lounger and sat down to wait. Finally he emerged from his room and came towards her.

'Ready to go?' They might have been business acquaintances, ready to share transport and only formally known to each other. Ben's dark face was cold and impassive, the scar etched clearly as if strained. Laura looked up at the harsh-faced stranger above her and nodded. She had been crazy to think she could make a friend—a lover—of this haunted man.

The 'phantom'. . . Kylie's name for him came flooding back, and with desolation Laura acknowledged that the label was apt. Even when he was with her, she didn't know him. He was driven by demons she could only guess at.

On impulse she put up her hand and touched his fingers.

'Don't worry,' she said softly. 'I'm not trying to intrude on your precious fortress. Take me back to Calua Bay and you can retreat to your ridge and never see me again.' Then she stood decisively, picked up her suitcase and walked swiftly to the hotel entrance,

trying to block back the tears that were threatening to
ruin her dignity.

Peter and Marie emerged from the office to bid them
farewell, but it was a brief meeting. There were other
patrons leaving and they could only spare a moment.

'Your skirt and blouse are in my room,' Laura told
Marie. 'Thank you. . .'

Marie looked into the younger girl's face and
frowned. She didn't like the look she saw there. And
Peter had reported that things were looking so
promising. . .

'Come back to see us soon,' she told Laura urgently.
Then she cast a swift glance across at Ben, ensuring he
was out of earshot. 'Don't let him drive you away,' she
said fiercely. 'He'll try. But Laura, he needs you.'

Laura stared at Marie for a long moment and then
shook her head. 'I don't think Ben Durell needs
anyone,' she said.

Zia's school was situated not more than a couple of
miles from Bellbyre Inn. As they pulled into the
beautifully manicured and spacious grounds of the
private school Laura forced herself to speak for the
first time.

'I'll stay in the car while you see your daughter,' she
suggested. 'Or I'll take a walk if you're a while.'

Ben pulled the Range Rover to a halt in the car park
beside the main entrance and turned to Laura. His
expression, if anything, had become even more set and
grim.

'Zia will be the first to tell you that she's not my
daughter,' he said harshly. 'She's the daughter of my
dead wife. And I know she'd appreciate you coming in
with me. She finds the interviews with me a strain.'

Laura frowned. 'Why?' she asked.

'I don't come up to her ideal of the perfect step-father. ' Ben was out of the car, reaching for his cane. 'I'd appreciate it if you came.'

He was already closing the door, and walking around to assist her from the passenger side. For a moment Laura toyed with the idea of refusing, but it was an idle thought. She could no more refuse anything of this man than fly to the moon. She shrugged and swung herself on to the gravel.

Ben's wife must have been beautiful. That was Laura's first thought when she met Zia for the first time. Summoned by the house mistress, the girl almost floated towards them, with a lightness and grace that told at once that here was another dancer in the making.

She might have only been fourteen, but there was no puppy fat on this child. Zia was exquisite, from the tip of her perfectly groomed, shining hair to the toes of her tiny feet. She made her school uniform seem an elegant and desirable outfit.

Laura and Ben had been ushered into one of the small reception-rooms to the right of the main entrance. The house mistress showed Zia in and closed the door behind her.

There was no fond greeting, Laura noticed.

'Hello,' Zia said formally, her mouth smiling but her eyes wary. She cast a quick glance up at Ben and then away, as if she could not bear to see. She looked to Laura, waiting for an introduction.

'This is Dr Haley,' Ben told her. 'Laura, my step-daughter, Zia.'

'Hi.' Zia came over and took Laura's hand. This

time, Laura noticed, her smile reached her eyes. She met Laura's eyes full on. 'It's nice of you to come to see me.'

'Ben dragged me in,' Laura confessed. She was feeling acutely uncomfortable. 'If you two want to talk, though. . .'

'Oh, no,' Zia said quickly. There was another uncomfortable darting glance at Ben. 'That is, I don't think my stepfather can have anything to say to me in private.'

Ben was watching her, his mouth set in a grim line. 'Would you like to come out to lunch, Zia?' he asked. 'We don't have to be back on Calua Bay until tonight.'

'Oh, no!' The words were an exclamation of rejection. And then she thought for a moment and it was obvious to both adults that she was looking for an excuse. 'I. . . I have to watch a tennis match between the senior girls this afternoon.'

Ben nodded as if he had expected no less. They chatted in a stilted, formal fashion for a couple more minutes, Zia responding as if she was performing a difficult duty.

Finally a silence fell. We can't leave already, Laura thought. This is ridiculous!

'The gardens around the school look lovely,' she suggested. 'How about showing me around, Zia?'

Zia looked uncertain and flashed another look at Ben. He rose and crossed to the door.

'I need to talk to the headmistress,' he said quietly. 'You can show Laura around without fear that any of your friends will see me, Zia.' He walked out and closed the door behind him.

Laura was left staring at the unrepentant girl. She was actually smiling and had also risen.

'Let's go, then,' she said to Laura. 'You're right, the gardens are lovely.'

Laura took a deep breath. She followed the girl out on to the lawns and didn't speak until she had collected her thoughts.

'Was Ben right?' she asked then, interrupting Zia's running commentary on the school facilities. 'Don't you like being seen with him?'

'He's very understanding,' Zia agreed. 'He knows it worries me dreadfully.'

'What worries you?'

Zia turned and stared at her. 'Why, his deformity, of course,' she said simply. 'It makes me feel sick. And I couldn't bear my friends to see.' She grinned. 'They think my father pays my school fees.'

'Your father. . .'

'My father's a choreographer now,' Zia said blithely. 'Not a very good one. He wanted me to dance in his last effort and I had to refuse. It wouldn't have done my ballet career the least bit of good. But the girls think he's fabulous because he used to be quite famous when he was dancing.'

Laura found that her hands were clenched into tight little balls and her nails were hurting her palms. This child, it seemed, had an almost boundless capacity to hurt.

'You know, Ben's not deformed,' she said quietly. 'He has a scar on his face and a limp. If you define that as deformed then you cut off a good section of the human race. I'm sure other of your school and ballet friends have physical imperfections.'

'Not my friends.' Zia raised a hand in greeting to a couple of girls walking by arm in arm. 'I can't bear it. I often wonder how Ben can bring himself to be seen in public.'

If he had to face people like Zia, Laura wondered at it herself. 'Aren't you fond of him?' she asked.

Zia shrugged. 'I suppose so,' she said. 'It's hard to be fond of someone when you feel sick every time you look at them.'

And it would be hard to be fond of someone who felt sick every time they saw you, Laura thought bitterly. No wonder Ben saw little of his stepdaughter. It was a wonder he still concerned himself with her at all. But then, he had loved her mother. . .

Ben came to find them a few moments later. Zia saw him coming and by the time he reached them she had adroitly changed course to be out of sight of any passing girls.

'Is that all?' she asked as he approached. 'I. . . I have to get ready for tennis.'

'I thought you were just watching?' Ben said drily. He turned to Laura. 'Would you like to stay and watch as well?'

Laura watched Zia's face turn to white. She felt an almost overwhelming compulsion to reach out and give the girl a good shake. Instead she shook her head.

'I think we'd better go,' she said.

Ben looked from Laura to Zia and nodded. 'Is there anything you need, Zia?'

'I could use some cash,' she said bluntly. 'I'm dancing in the lead of my class concert next month and the costume's expensive. My father can't afford it.'

Ben nodded. 'I'll send a cheque in the mail.'

'Thanks. Goodbye, then.' Still she didn't look at him. She turned to Laura and smiled. 'It was nice meeting you.' Then she was off, flying over the lawn on nimble feet, eager to get as far from them as possible.

'Duty done for the term,' Ben said harshly. He was staring after her.

'Yours or hers,' Laura asked. They turned and walked towards the car park.

'Both.' Ben shrugged. 'I'm not sure who hates it most.'

'She's a foolish child,' Laura said softly. She cast a look up to Ben's face and could see, through the forbidding countenance, the hurt reflected in his dark eyes.

'She's getting better.' They reached the Range Rover and Ben assisted Laura in before going around to start the engine. 'She used to scream every time she saw me.'

'Oh, Ben. . .'

'For God's sake, don't feel sorry for me!' His words were an angry rebuttal. 'I've had enough of that to last a lifetime.'

'I don't.'

He cast a startled glance at her, but Laura didn't elaborate. She sat back against the luxurious leather seat and was silent.

CHAPTER NINE

THEY arrived back in Calua Bay late that afternoon. It was a tense trip across the mountains and Laura was relieved to come around the last mountainous curve to see Calua Bay and the wide sweep of blue-green sea before them.

She cast a worried glance across at Ben. He had been silent and grim all the way back and seemed now as aloof from her as he would be back in his fortress out on Blackwood Ridge.

'Are you going home tonight?' she asked softly. He flicked a glance across at her.

'Unless you can create any more dramas,' he said roughly, and Laura flinched.

'You make it sound as if I set you up.'

He shrugged. 'You did, in a way,' he said coldly. 'You know you can't manage the medical practice here on your own.'

'I know that now,' Laura agreed, swallowing the feeling of desolation flooding through her. 'I'll contact Cliff Paige this week and tell him if he doesn't come back I'm not interested in the job long-term.'

'And you'll leave.' It was a statement, not a question.

'Yes.'

'So Calua Bay will be without a doctor.'

'Cliff Paige may come back.'

Ben shook his head. 'If Cliff Paige comes back to this town he faces the medical board,' he said quietly. 'I've checked those damned files. Sunset Lodge has been running on an "I'll scratch your back, you scratch mine" basis for years between Paige and the Palmers. With the amount of sedative being prescribed I'd be almost sure of having him struck off, and as well as that he's been charging for examinations I'm damned sure haven't been performed.'

Laura looked down at her hands. 'I can't stay here,' she said quietly. 'I'm not experienced enough to cope, and if I leave then the town has a chance of getting a married doctor team. It's probably the only chance the town has of finding two doctors.'

Ben nodded. 'You're right there.'

There was silence again as Ben negotiated the streets up to the hospital. Finally they pulled up outside Laura's apartment.

'Will you. . .will you come in?' Laura looked across and bit her lip. She was sounding like a gauche schoolgirl. Ben nodded without smiling.

'I'd better find out what's happened to Rod,' he said.

For a radiologist, Rod had performed exceedingly well. He emerged from the hospital to greet them.

'Well, well. . .' He was a big fair man with an infectious smile. 'If it's not our truants.' He mock-punched Ben on the shoulder. 'It's the last time I drop in on you,' he threatened. Then he turned to Laura and raised his eyebrows. 'Dr Haley, I presume.' He looked again at his friend and smiled. 'All of a sudden things are becoming clearer. . .'

Laura flushed. The implication behind his words was obvious.

'I'm sorry you were landed with my work,' she said. 'I hope it was quiet.'

'It wasn't quiet at all,' he told her. 'I was crazy

enough to run a clinic this morning. It lasted until three this afternoon.'

'Oh, no.' Laura flushed with guilt. 'It's because they'll all be interested in a different doctor.'

'I get the definite feeling that nobody in this town knows what the hell is going on with the medical fraternity,' Rod told her. 'I've never fielded so many questions.' Then he smiled again. 'I thought up some terrific answers too. The local gossips have enough material to keep them going for a month.'

Laura smiled but her smile was strained. 'No real drama?' she queried.

'Only Mrs Finlayson,' Rod admitted. 'Meg was five minutes late with her cocoa last night and by the time she'd blasted the poor girl to her satisfaction she'd worked herself up to such a frenzy that she had a heart attack. She died half an hour later.'

'Oh, Rod!' Laura stared in horror.

'It was no more than she deserved,' Rod said ruthlessly. 'I examined her earlier in the night and she threatened to have me sacked because my hands were cold.' He shrugged. 'I gather she was eighty-six. She had Meg in tears, and what more can an old harridan ask for? She died happy, in the knowledge that she'd made the people around her miserable to the last. I hand back with pleasure and admiration, Dr Haley. Give me my nice quiet X-ray department any day.'

'I'm so sorry,' Laura said contritely, and Rod smiled at her with reassurance.

'To be strictly truthful, I almost enjoyed it,' he confessed. 'Especially knowing there was an end in sight.' He looked around the back of the Range Rover to where Ben was unloading Laura's suitcase. 'Tom Burne left a message,' he told him. 'He's trying to get things sorted out down at Sunset Lodge. He said if you weren't back too late, could you go down there before you go back out to the ridge?' Then Rod looked back at Laura. 'And I'm going to have to get some help with Mrs Finlayson's paperwork before I leave you,' he told her. 'I must be the world's best radiologist, I reckon. I haven't filled in a death certificate for years.'

'I'll go down to Sunset Lodge now,' Ben told them. 'If I get things sorted out with Tom tonight I won't have to come in again. If you finish up here, Rod, I'll pick you up in an hour. Then we'll go out and have that beer you demanded when you arrived.'

'It's probably gone stale by now,' Rod said morosely. Then he brightened. 'Still, there are worse things in life than stale beer. Another twenty-four hours in this place, for instance.'

It took twenty minutes for Rod and Laura to cope with the paperwork associated with Mrs Finlayson's death, and for Rod to hand back over the patients in the hospital. Most of them greeted Laura with bemusement, and Laura couldn't blame them. After five years of seeing no other doctor than Cliff Paige, to have three different doctors in a week was enough to confuse the calmest patient.

Alice greeted Laura with delight. 'I'm going home on Monday,' she told Laura proudly. 'Tom's taking the week off.'

'So he's definitely taking on Sunset Lodge?' Laura smiled.

'Oh, yes.' Alice hesitated and then returned Laura's smile. 'He's missed nursing so much, but he couldn't go back into mainstream critical care. And he's going to be in charge. I don't know how to thank you. . .'

'Thank Dr Durell,' Laura said honestly. 'I wouldn't have thought of it.'

'Because we were dopes with the baby?' Alice shrugged and looked down into the crib beside the bed. 'I can't believe we took such a stupid risk.' She looked up at Laura and Rod. 'Believe me, though, we've learned our lesson. Doctors have their uses.'

'It's lovely to hear such appreciation,' Rod grinned. 'Next thing she'll be knitting us socks.'

'I will if you like,' Alice promised. 'With home-spun wool.'

'Complete with burrs?' Rod asked, and then, as Alice smiled and nodded, he shook his head decisively. 'Save your gratitude for Dr Durell, my dear,' he told her kindly. 'He deserves it.'

Laura picked up the obs chart from the end of the bed and frowned. She looked up at Alice. Was it her imagination or was the girl white-faced? She put the chart back and went back to the bed.

'How are you feeling?' she asked.

'Actually, I'm a bit headachy,' the girl confessed. 'Tom's got the mother and father of a head cold and I'm starting to think I might be coming down with it as well.'

Tactfully Rod drifted away, and Laura did a swift examination. There was nothing to explain the slight temperature rise. Alice could be right, Laura thought with sympathy. A heavy head cold would be all the girl needed.

'If you're right we might keep you in a day or two longer,' Laura told her. 'I want you fit before you're coping with young Sam on your own.'

'Yes, ma'am,' Alice told her, and Laura smiled. Alice had certainly changed her tune.

With the change-over done, Laura and Rod made their way back to Laura's apartment. There was no sign of Ben. Laura made coffee, and then by mutual consent they went out on to the front steps to drink it. The sun was going down behind the mountains, and the dusky pink hues of sunset were scattered all around them. The ocean looked still and serene in the distance.

'It's a lovely spot,' Rod said as they settled themselves on to the step.

'Mm. It's a pity I can't stay,' Laura told him. Then, at his enquiring look, she found herself telling this sympathetic stranger about the medical set-up of the town.

'I can't cope,' she finished. 'Not on my own.'

'And Ben won't help?'

Laura smiled without humour. 'What do you think?' she said quietly. 'He's a specialist obstetrician, for heaven's sake, besides being adamant that he'll no longer practise.'

'He's still left with scars that need healing,' Rod said quietly. He looked across at the girl beside him and nodded as though coming to a decision. There was pain in those big green eyes that could not be totally explained by having to leave this place. And he had seen the way she looked at his friend.

'I knew Ben well before the accident,' he said quietly. 'We went through uni together, and then did our residency in the same hospital. I was best man at his wedding.'

Laura didn't speak. She wasn't sure that Rod should be talking to her like this, and she didn't know whether she should be listening.

'The marriage was foundering well before the accident,' Rod said slowly. He cast a careful look at Laura before continuing. She just as carefully avoided his gaze. 'Claire was an entrancing creature, but she was obsessed with her body. It was an illness in the end.' He shrugged. 'But then, you've met Zia,' he said. 'If you've seen Zia then you've seen Claire. Imagine a Zia whose body wasn't quite what she regarded as perfect.'

Laura nodded. 'She'd have no resources to fall back on.'

Rod nodded. 'She hurt Ben dreadfully. And then, when she died, her daughter inflicted more pain.'

'I've seen it,' Laura said slowly.

Rod shook his head. 'You've seen a faint trace of it,' he said. 'Zia was eight when her mother died. Her father was out of the country and there was only Ben. Marie and Peter took her in until Ben was near recovered.' He grimaced. 'I was with Ben when Marie brought Zia to see him for the first time.'

'I. . . I think I can imagine,' Laura said, thinking back to the girl she had met.

Rod shook his head. 'No, you can't,' he said savagely. 'Here was a man who had just seen his wife die in a car accident, and was dreadfully injured himself. He felt responsible for Zia—her father doesn't seem to give a damn about her—and all Zia would do was scream the roof off every time she came near Ben. It reached the stage where Zia would make herself ill rather than go to the hospital, and it's scarcely improved. Zia tolerates Ben because without him she can't have the best school and the best dancing masters. And that's it.'

Laura nodded. 'Is that why he's decided on a reclusive life? Has it affected him that much?'

Rod shook his head. 'Not entirely,' he went on. 'His texts were doing well, and with his flair for astute investment there was no need to practise. He would have continued, though, if it hadn't been for his first two patients after he started back at work. Both were expectant mothers with toddlers. Ben walked into the waiting-room, one of the toddlers took one look at Ben's scarred face and started doing a Zia impersonation. The other kid followed suit. Ben walked out and has never been back.'

'That's ridiculous,' Laura said softly. 'Kids scream at anything.'

'I know,' Rod said grimly. 'Try and tell that to Ben, though. He doesn't need to expose himself, and he doesn't see why he should.' He smiled across at Laura. 'I've given it my best shot. Now it's your turn.'

Laura shook her head. 'You're his friend,' she told the man beside her. 'If you can't help, what can I do?'

Rod grinned. 'If I told Ben he was damned attractive he'd look at me sideways. But if you were to do it. . .' He left the statement unfinished and turned away. There was a vehicle approaching up the hill, and in a matter of moments the Range Rover was pulling into the car park.

Ben came to a halt and swung out of the driver's seat. Laura was interested to note that he no longer bothered to reach back for the cane. Even a week's enforced exercise had helped.

'Ready?' he asked Rod.

'When you are.'

Ben nodded. 'There's just Dr Haley's stitches,' he said briefly. 'I should have asked you to take the things out while I was away.'

Rod held up his hands in mock-horror. 'Hell, no,' he grinned. 'I faint at the sight of blood. That's why I'm a radiologist.'

'I'll ask Sister Carter to do it,' Laura said stiffly. 'She's quite capable.'

Ben shook his head. 'Come on,' he said brusquely. He started walking over to the casualty entrance. 'Are you coming to watch, Rod?'

'I'll listen to the screams from a distance,' Rod promised.

It took very little time for the stitches to be removed. Laura sat on a chair in an examination cubicle and tried to blot out the feel of the strong, probing fingers on her forehead. For some reason she was getting closer and closer to tears.

Finally it was finished. Ben laid the small scissors down and nodded. 'You'll do,' he said brusquely.

'Thank you.' Laura looked up at him. 'I. . . Thank you for coming to fetch me.'

He looked down at her, his dark eyes expressionless. 'There's no need to thank me. You've paid your debts. . .'

Laura gasped. 'Because I slept with you?' she said stiffly.

'That's not what I meant.'

'Isn't it?' She rose, holding on to the arm of the chair. She was feeling a little sick. She looked up at Ben's cold face and, deep within, anger stirred. 'Why do you think I slept with you, Ben Durell?' she asked softly. And then her voice grew louder. 'Just why the hell do you think I slept with you?'

Ben shrugged. 'Who knows?' he said evenly. 'Because you were alone and missing your fiancé. Because you were grateful. . . Because you felt sorry for me. . .'

Laura took a step back and glared. 'You know, Ben

Durell, for a supercilious, arrogant male you can sometimes be really stupid.'

His face was expressionless, closed and shuttered against her. His skin was stretched tight over the fading scar, and he seemed, all at once, very tired. Tired and vulnerable, Laura thought suddenly. She ached for the harsh expression to fade, and for the courage to put her hands up and smooth the lines of pain.

'Well, why?' he said evenly.

Laura took a deep breath. How could she say it? How could she find the courage to say the words?

And in the end it was only because she was angry that the words came. It was only because he had accused her of using her body for payment.

'I would never sleep with you because I felt sorry for you, or grateful or alone,' she said, and her voice shook with unshed tears. 'I slept with you because I'm in love with you, Ben. And you can do with that what you like, Ben Durell. You can do with that what you like. . .'

There was dead silence between them. Laura felt her eyes welling over with tears, but she was incapable of brushing them away. Damn him. . . Damn the man. . . Why didn't he say something?

Then he reached out and touched her wisping bright curls, a feather touch.

'Don't do this to yourself, Laura,' he told her harshly. 'Whatever you say, it's a form of sympathy and I can't bear it.'

Laura looked up through her tears and gasped. Sympathy? Sympathy?

'Don't be so bloody stupid,' she gasped. 'If you think I don't know the difference between sympathy and pure, gut-wrenching love then you're a fool, Ben

Durell. And you can go to hell. You can get in your precious Range Rover and get out of here, back to your splendid isolation on Blackwood Ridge. You can get lost!'

Still he didn't move. He stayed, his large body looming over hers, his eyes hooded and fathomless.

Go away, Laura's mind was screaming at him. Go away or take me. I've laid myself wide open for you. I've done everything I can do. Take me or go.

He went. With a sudden curse he wheeled around and left her staring forlornly after him.

The door of Casualty swung open and closed again after him. Laura heard the sound of Rod's voice, Ben's curt reply, and then the engine of the Range Rover gunned into life.

She stayed quite still until she could hear it no longer. Then, at the sound of an approaching nurse, she fled to the sanctuary of her own apartment.

The rest of the weekend passed like a bad dream. Laura functioned on automatic pilot, performing her duties with mechanical care. There was the Sunday-morning clinic, quieter than usual, Laura thought, as most patients with any symptom at all had used it to see Rod the day before, the hospital patients and the occasional casualty patient.

There were also Mrs Finlayson's relatives to counsel. They emerged from nowhere—a daughter and two sons, none of whom had been near their mother for months, full of easy sorrow and remorse. Laura found herself, for the first time, feeling sympathy for the old lady, but then she reminded herself of Mrs Finlayson's wicked tongue and asked herself which had come first—the old lady's ability to inflict hurt or the family's alienation. It was impossible to tell.

Alice was still not well, and Laura found herself drifting into the room at odd times during the day to check the girl. Her temperature was still raised, but there was no sign of the promised head cold.

If it's not down by this evening I'll put up an antibiotic drip anyway, Laura promised herself. She didn't want any complications now.

Late afternoon the place settled down. For the first time there was nothing to do. She could catch up on her paperwork, but there was no way she could settle. Finally she slipped on her bathing costume, told the charge nurse where she could be found and drove down to the cove.

The water was balm to her overwrought mind. She slipped into the cool wash of the waves with gratitude, swam strongly out past the surf and lay back to float lazily in the afternoon sun.

Nearer the shore children were still laughing and splashing in the waves, but the noise did not disturb her. It was a perfect background for the scene around her.

She loved this place. She had been here for less than a month and she loved it. It would be heart-wrenching to leave it.

And more heart-wrenching to leave Ben. She opened her eyes and watched a gull wheel lazily overhead. What had he done to her to make herself feel so committed—so exposed? He had demanded nothing of her. Ross and her mother—their demands had been unrelenting. And here was a man who merely had to look at her through his dark, questioning eyes and she was his. And when he smiled, and the harsh austerity of his countenance softened. . . Laura's heart twisted within her and she felt her body contract as if in pain.

In desperation she rolled over and started swimming, up and down along the back of the surf, with long, even strokes that took all her energy. She was seeking to drive the image of him out of her mind.

Half an hour later she gave up. She was exhausted and the pain was no less relentless. She was like a small animal caught in a trap, unable to escape the pain.

She had to get away. It was the only path to go. Everything pointed to her leaving this place as fast as she could, and starting again.

And go where? She didn't have a clue. And it doesn't matter, her heart told her. Any place without Ben will be the same. Any place. . .

CHAPTER TEN

LAURA had been back at her apartment for fifteen minutes when the charge nurse rang through. She emerged from the shower, towelling her hair, to the sound of the phone.

'Mrs Burne's temperature is up to forty point two,' the girl said with concern. 'I thought you ought to know.'

'I'll be right over,' Laura said.

She dressed swiftly and ran a comb through her unruly damp curls, then walked quickly over to Alice's ward.

There was no denying that Alice was unwell. Her pulse had quickened and her skin was clammy. She looked up at Laura with worried eyes.

'It is just a cold, isn't it?' she asked. By her tone, Laura knew that the girl herself was no longer confident.

'I don't know,' Laura told her honestly. 'But I'm taking no chances. If you've copped an infection I want it nipped in the bud now.' She turned away and gave swift orders for a drip to be set up.

With antibiotic being administered intravenously there was little more she could do. Little except worry, she thought as she went back to her rooms. She made herself some soup and toast, and then didn't have the appetite to eat it. She hated this responsibility. This was why the local women were advised to have their

babies in Canberra, where there were facilities if things
went wrong.

She slept badly, rising periodically to go over to the
hospital and check Alice. Alice too was having a fitful
night.

The antibiotics should be working by morning, Laura
thought. If not. . .

Let that wait, Laura told herself firmly. There was
no point worrying over something that mightn't
eventuate.

It was almost as if she welcomed the worry, she
realised. Worrying about Alice kept her mind from
Ben, and she desperately needed the distraction.

It didn't work. There was little sleep for her, and she
rose soon after dawn feeling as if she hadn't been to
bed at all.

Monday! Laura dressed with a leaden feeling of
anticipation in the pit of her stomach. There was so
much work waiting for her that she didn't know where
to start, and this week there would be no Ben Durell
to lift the load from her shoulders. She was on her
own.

She abandoned her morning swim. Any more physical exercise and she'd go to sleep where she stood, she
thought, and, besides, she was concerned about Alice.
She did a careful ward-round, catching up on things
that had been done quickly over the weekend, and
ended up in Alice's ward.

The girl was no better, and as Laura checked her
discharge her heart sank. Instead of lightening, the
bleeding was becoming heavier. There was an infection
that would have to be cleared by a D and C.

'It means Canberra, I'm afraid,' Laura told the
worried girl in the bed. 'It has to be done under a

general anaesthetic, and I can't do that here. Not without help.'

'But what about Dr Durell?' Alice was very close to tears. The infection was taking its toll on her.

'He helped out in an emergency, but this isn't an emergency,' Laura told her. 'There's plenty of time to get you over the mountains. And Sam can go too.' Laura smiled down at the sleeping baby. 'It's not as if we're going to separate you from your precious son.'

'But I don't want to go to Canberra.' Alice was crying in earnest. 'Oh, why does everything have to go wrong? I don't want to go to a big city hospital. I want to stay here. Can't you ask Dr Durell?'

Laura bit her lip. Ben's words echoed back to her. 'Unless you can create any more dramas,' he had said. She sighed helplessly. This wasn't a drama. She couldn't ask for his help again.

'I can't,' she said gently. 'Dr Durell isn't practising, and he only delivered Sam because it was a matter of life and death. He's made it very clear that he doesn't want to be involved again. I'm afraid you're going to have to face the trip to the city.'

Alice stared at her for a long moment. Finally she turned away and hid her tear-drenched face in her pillows. 'Will you tell Tom?' she said through her tears.

Laura knew where Tom would be. He was working down at Sunset Lodge, trying to get the place into order before he needed to take time off to be with Alice when she and the baby came home. For a moment Laura considered ringing him, and then glanced at her watch. If she hurried she had time to go down there before morning clinic, and she wanted to see what was happening at the lodge. She drove down the hill with a heavy heart. She didn't want to send Alice away, but there seemed no help for it.

Two minutes later she pulled into the grounds of Sunset Lodge and stopped the car in amazement. Two weeks ago she had come here at the same time in the morning and had been greeted by deserted grounds and closed doors. This place was a hive of activity.

There were people everywhere. There were people sitting on the veranda, chatting to each other and enjoying the warmth of the sun before it reached its midday searing heat. There were people digging and weeding in the gardens beneath the veranda, and, above the front door, there were two elderly gentlemen on ladders attacking the sign 'Sunset Lodge' with screwdrivers and jemmies.

As Laura walked towards them Tom emerged from the front door.

'Have a care,' he laughed to the men on the ladder. 'If you break your necks you'll have me sacked.' He saw Laura and smiled. 'Whoops! Sprung!' He walked down the steps towards her, and Laura couldn't believe the change from the frightened man she had met at the birth of his son and this self-confident, laughing professional. 'Now we'll be in trouble for using cheap labour,' he grinned. He motioned to the sign. 'The problem is, if we wait for the carpenters then the name can't be changed for another week, and the residents want it changed now.'

'What are you changing it to?' Laura asked, smiling.

'We still haven't decided,' Tom confessed. 'We're having a vote over lunch. Calua View looks like winning, but there's a strong move for Sword's Sheath.'

'Sword's Sheath?' Laura wrinkled her nose in perplexity.

'We have a romantic in our midst,' Tom grinned. 'She reckons this is the place where battles cease, though going on the home's history over the last fortnight I'm not too sure.'

Laura shook her head. 'I can't believe this is the same place.'

'Ben did a reivew of all medication while you were away,' Tom told her. 'The change here is incredible. It's like it's waking up after an over-long sleep. Some of these people seem to have shed ten years. Mind,' he said reflectively, 'the night staff don't know what's hit them. We've had to triple staff.'

'Can the place afford it?'

'If the amount the Palmers have been siphoning off can be ploughed back into the place there's no stopping us,' Tom grinned. 'Plus the fact that it seems some of the money may well be recoverable.'

Laura nodded, and then took a deep breath. The sun was warm on her face and Tom was content. She didn't want to break the spell, but she had no choice.

'Tom, I need to talk to you about Alice,' she said quietly. Swiftly she outlined the problems, reassuring him as she did. 'You know as well as I that this sometimes happens,' she told him. 'It's just a matter of clearing the infected matter.'

'I understand that,' Tom said slowly. 'But surely she doesn't need to go to Canberra?'

'I can't give a general anaesthetic,' Laura told him. 'Not by myself.'

'I understand that. But won't Ben come down?'

'He's made it clear he wants no further involvement in the place,' Laura said firmly. 'I can't ask him.'

Tom stared at her for a long moment. 'Alice isn't going to Canberra to save our pride,' he said shortly.

'She's already treating herself as if she's failed by not having the baby at home. If you won't ask him then I will.'

'Tom, you can't.'

He shook his head at her. His new job had given him a confidence that hung over him like a mantle. 'Watch me,' he said. He turned and called to a woman on the veranda. A middle-aged, genial-faced woman came down the steps towards them.

'This is Mrs Christy,' Tom told Laura. 'She was a supervisor here before the Palmers took over and sacked her, and she's a trained nurse. She's agreed to be second in command here.' He turned to the approaching woman and performed a quick introduction. 'I'll be away for the morning,' he told the woman. 'OK?'

'We'll get on fine,' Mrs Christy beamed. 'Especially. . .' She motioned to the doorway, where the men were descending from the ladder with the remains of the sign in their hands. 'Especially since they've finished.'

'Tom, you can't,' Laura said urgently. 'It will look as if I'm screaming for help again.'

'I'm thinking of Alice,' Tom said brusquely. 'I'm sorry, Dr Haley, but if I can talk him into it I don't see that you have any choice in the matter. You agree that it would be better to operate here?'

'Yes,' Laura agreed. 'But——'

'Then there's no more to be said.' Tom was already moving towards his disreputable panel van. 'I'll let you know what's happening. Damn the man for not having the phone on.'

There was nothing else for Laura to do but return to

the hospital and start morning clinic. Kylie welcomed her with delight.

'Welcome back,' she told her. 'What's going to happen this week?'

'Nothing,' Laura said with feeling. 'Absolutely nothing. I want a really boring week. Just see to it, will you, Kylie? If anyone presents you with anything more dramatic than in ingrown toenail, call the ambulance and send them to Canberra.'

She worked solidly, seeing one patient after another, but all the time her mind was on Tom and the outcome of his visit to Blackwood Ridge. If she hadn't heard by midday she was going to have to send Alice anyway, she decided. The operation could wait until this evening but she didn't want to wait any longer.

Finally, in the middle of a diatribe on the evils of Mr Patterson's snoring, the phone rang. Laura cast an apologetic smile across to Mrs Patterson and answered it. It was Tom.

'He'll be down at two this afternoon,' Tom told her, his voice containing a hint of triumph.

'Oh, Tom. . .' Laura stared down at the phone. 'Was he angry?'

'Yes,' Tom admitted. 'To be honest, he refused. And then I lost my temper and told him if he didn't help he could find someone else to run his retirement home.'

'You didn't. . . Tom, you really want that job. . .'

'More than he needs me,' Tom agreed. 'But it made him see I was in deadly earnest. Anyway, he doesn't like it, but he's doing it.'

Laura nodded. She could see Ben's reasoning, though. Once the locals knew he was available he would be inundated with requests that were all reasonable. Alice's need was only the first. Laura had opened the floodgate, as far as Ben was concerned, and she had no doubt the blame would be laid squarely at her feet.

Mrs Patterson was watching with barely concealed impatience, and with a sigh Laura bade Tom farewell and put the phone down. She let Kylie know of the impending surgery and left the arrangements to her, then turned her attention back to the imperatives of the snoring spouse.

When Ben arrived everything was ready. Laura had left nothing to chance. If he had to come then she could at least see that he would not have to wait. The theatre was ready and Alice given her pre-med.

'Thank you,' Alice said as she was wheeled into Theatre. 'This means a lot to me, you know.'

'You can thank your husband,' Laura told the girl. 'I had no say in it at all.' Not that Ben would believe that, of course. They had started their acquaintance with anger, and were doomed to finish it the same way, she thought.

He arrived three minutes before two o'clock, striding into the hospital with only a trace of a limp. Anger's good for him, Laura thought briefly. It makes him use his leg. Then she met his angry eyes and her thoughts faltered. Her heart cringed. How could she bear him looking at her like that?

'Are you ready?' It was an angry snap, and Laura nodded unhappily.

'Yes.' She felt like a very junior resident being caught in some misdeed. Briefly she outlined the history, and Ben nodded. He picked up the chart and glanced at the obs.

'Well, at least I'm not here for nothing,' he growled.

Then he approached the trolley where Alice lay in drowsy anticipation.

'Well, Mrs Burne, let's see if we can get things right this time.'

It was as if he was a different man, Laura thought in wonder. He smiled down at Alice and even made her laugh. Then he left briefly to scrub, while Laura administered the general anaesthetic.

It took very little time. The procedure was straight-forward with no complications, and Laura sighed with relief as it was completed. Finally the stirrups were released and Laura was able to reverse the anaesthetic.

'She'll do now,' Ben said briefly. 'Though she could have done without this.' It was the first time he had talked to Laura as if she were human, and Laura's colour deepened. She looked up from what she was doing, but Ben's look was still forbidding, stopping any attempt at conversation on her part. She bit her lip and bent again over the anaesthetic trolley.

Alice was just starting to come around when the door of Theatre opened. It was Meg, the only member of staff not in Theatre.

'There's a little boy in Casualty,' she told Laura. 'His parents have just brought him in. He was hit by a surfboard and his arm looks horrid.' She looked down at the stirring Alice and frowned. 'What should I do?'

Ben moved towards the anaesthetic trolley and motioned to Laura that he take over. 'I'll do this,' he told her. 'I don't want to get involved again.' His accent was heavily on the 'again', and Laura flushed.

She cast one glance down at Alice but Ben was right. He could manage himself now. There was no need for her to stay. By the sound of the sobbing starting to echo through the hospital, there was a more urgent need for her in Casualty.

The child was three or four, dressed in bathers and wrapped in a towel. His parents were also in beach gear and looked at once frightened and uncomfortable.

'He's broken his arm,' the young mother told Laura, her voice trembling. 'It looks awful.'

The child was in his father's arms, cringing as close as he could get to his father's body.

'Can you turn him around so I can see?' Laura asked gently. She turned to the mother. 'What's his name?'

'Joshua.'

Laura put a hand on the child's back, touching him gently. 'Let me see your arm, Joshua,' she said. 'I'm a doctor and I'm good at fixing sore arms.'

The child turned his head, gave Laura one long, angry stare and started to scream.

'Go away! Go away from Joshua. Take her away. Get her away, Daddy.'

The father cast Laura an apologetic glance and tried to prise his son from his shoulder. The boy's screams escalated.

'No. No. No. She's a witch, Daddy. Get her away. I don't want her. I want to go back to the beach.'

'Josh, this is silly.'

The mother's words only aggravated the child. He started kicking, thrashing against his father, and the movement hurt his arm more, making him scream with increasing intensity.

It was every doctor's nightmare. The child was injured and needed to be seen, but if the screaming didn't stop he was going to make himself sick. Laura took a deep breath.

'Joshua!'

He swung wildly and slapped out with his good hand, screaming as the movement hurt his shoulder. 'Go away. Go away. Joshua hates you. Go away!'

'What on earth is all this fuss?'

The low, deep tone from the doorway made Laura start and even gave Joshua pause. Acting on a momentary advantage, Ben crossed the room, lifted the child decisively from the grasp of his startled parents, signalled them with his eyes to leave the room and then placed the stunned child on the examination couch. The whole process took perhaps five seconds, and even Laura was open-mouthed at the end of it.

Joshua gaped up at the man who had treated him in such a cavalier fashion and opened his mouth to scream again.

'I wouldn't,' Ben advised. 'Did you know that we've a very sick lady in the next room, Joshua, and your screaming is frightening her? Besides, there's nothing to scream about.' His fingers were doing a fast examination as he talked. Now that the child was no longer huddled against his father, Laura could see clearly what the problem was. The shoulder wasn't broken. It was merely dislocated.

'Did a surfboard do this?' Ben asked with interest. 'It must have been a big surfboard. Did you see it?'

'It was red,' Joshua sniffed. 'Don't let the lady come near me. She's ugly.'

Ben looked around at Laura and grinned. 'I can't say I agree with your taste, young man, but if you say so I'll protect you from her. Did you say she was a witch?'

'She eats children,' Joshua announced with authority. 'I want my mummy.'

'She'll be back in a moment,' Ben promised. He had

his hands in position, felt for resistance, took a deep
breath and pulled. The shoulder slid effortlessly back
into place.

Joshua gave a scream, but it was more of indignation
than of pain. He pulled his small person away from
Ben and glared. Ben smiled and rumpled his hair.

'Sorry about that,' he told him. He signalled Meg to
fetch in the parents. 'I've just fixed your arm, though,
and I'll bet it feels a whole heap better.'

Joshua was admitting no such thing. He grabbed his
arm and glowered. Then his father reached him. From
the safe haven of his father's arms he sobbed out his
indignation.

'It's fixed,' Ben reassured the parents. 'It was just a
simple dislocation.'

The mother looked helplessly at her son and then
across to Laura. 'I'm so sorry,' she stammered. 'He
doesn't usually. . . He's not usually so rude.'

'He was in pain,' Laura smiled. 'And children in pain
or under stress react in different ways. We were just
lucky Dr Durell was here.' She risked a glance up at
Ben. 'And for some reason he didn't think Ben looked
like a warlock.'

The child's father had succeeded in turning his son
around. 'Thank the doctors,' he ordered the little boy.
Reassured that his son was OK, he obviously thought
it wise to restore some semblance of control over the
situation.

'I'll thank him,' Joshua said grimly, pointing at Ben.
'But I won't thank her. She's got red hair!'

Ben grinned and nodded. 'It's hard to see how some
people rather like it,' he smiled. 'One man's meat. . .'
Then he laughed, and told the parents to take their

little boy home. 'Before he thinks of something worse to say,' he told them. 'And Joshua?'

'Yes?' The little boy eyed him suspiciously.

'I'd avoid red surfboards in future. They're much, much worse than redheaded doctors.'

Then they were gone and Meg followed them out. For a moment they were silent. Ben was still smiling.

'I'd better go,' Laura said quietly, glancing at her watch. She had patients booked from two-thirty and it was after that now. 'Is Alice OK?'

'Fully conscious and back in the ward,' Ben reassured her. 'Tom's with her.'

'I'm sorry you were called.'

'It seems you can't do without me,' he quizzed her, and Laura flushed.

'I would have managed Joshua,' she said stiffly.

'What's the bet he'd still be a screaming heap with a dislocated shoulder?' Ben said. He had folded his arms and was watching her with enjoyment.

Laura flushed. 'At least I stuck around,' she retorted hotly. 'I didn't take umbrage, pack my bags and go and find myself a ridge to sit on for the rest of my life, like some people I know.' She stalked out with as much dignity as she could muster, banging the door behind her.

CHAPTER ELEVEN

To LAURA'S relief, the rest of the week was quiet.
Alice settled down to recover, and on Thursday was
finally fit to go home.

'Come up to the farm and see where we live,' she
begged Laura. 'We'll be sending you an invitation to
the christening.'

'I don't know whether I'll still be here then,' Laura
said slowly. She had tried several times to contact Cliff
Paige with no success, but it was up to him to advertise
her job. Legally the Calua Bay practice was still his.
With no way to contact him, and an agreement to stay
until he heard about the exam, she was feeling trapped.

'Well, come and see us wherever you end up,' Alice
told her. 'If you have to travel we can put you up for
the weekend.'

'I'll see where I am,' Laura hedged. The knowledge
that for a certainty Ben Durell would be an invited
guest as well made her hesitate. Once she left here, she
didn't want any contact to wrench at her heart again.

How long does it take to fall out of love? she
wondered. She didn't have a clue. Her pain was
growing deeper rather than less, and it had only been
three days since she had seen the man.

She bade Alice goodbye and settled down to work,
and in work at least she could drive away some of the
demons.

Friday was the last day of the school summer holiday
and Laura's Saturday-morning clinic fell away dramati-

cally as the tourists packed up and left the little town. On Saturday afternoon, for the first time since she had come back to Calua Bay, she had time on her hands.

The sensation was so novel that it was almost unpleasant. Laura wandered around her little apartment feeling vaguely guilty. She had risen early and gone for a swim, and couldn't justify to her conscience going back to the beach. Besides, she was becoming altogether too attached to her daily swim. When she left she faced the possibility of finding an inland practice, and the thought didn't appeal one bit.

Laura picked up a book and went out to sit on her front step to read. The words danced up and down before her eyes. She looked down the hill at the distant ocean and her eyes filled with tears. Life was just so damnably unfair. She had wanted this job to work so much.

She would have to go indoors. She couldn't sit here and look at all she was going to miss. Calua Bay—the name was synonymous with Ben Durell, and both were enough to tear her apart. She rose, and as she did the sound of a vehicle turning into the hospital car park made her hesitate.

The car park was filled with the vehicles belonging to hospital visitors, but this car didn't seem to fit with the rest. It was a sleek, shining Rover. Laura watched as it drew to a halt, and Ben's radiologist friend, Rod, unwound himself from the dirver's seat. From the passenger seat emerged a younger version of Rod.

Rod beamed a welcome with characteristic good humour. 'We're a bit late,' he grinned. 'I'm glad you waited.'

'Waited?' Laura smiled and took Rod's outstretched hand. 'Was I expecting you?'

'Me, no,' Rod grinned. 'But surely my brother here.'
He gestured towards the younger man and performed
an introduction. 'Laura, this is my younger brother,
Pete. Pete, meet Dr Haley.'

The younger man gave a smile to match Rod's. 'It
was OK, Rod bringing me up?' he asked. 'Ben said
there was a hospital car.'

Laura gave up smiling and her brow creased in
perplexity. 'A hospital car,' she said blankly.

'For the doctor.' Pete was looking at her as if she
were slightly dense.

'Yes,' Laura said slowly. 'There's a hospital car, but
I drive my own. I don't see. . .'

'That's all right, then.' Pete's brow cleared. 'Ben will
have told you I'm just back from a year in the UK. I
haven't got around to buying a car yet.'

There was a drawn-out silence. The men were clearly
expecting Laura to respond. Finally she spread her
hands helplessly in front of her. 'I'm sorry,' she said.
'But I haven't the faintest idea what is going on.'

Rod and Pete looked at each other. Then they
looked at Laura. Finally Rod sighed.

'That's what you get for leaving things to another
party,' he sighed. He looked at Laura and smiled. 'Dr
Haley, meet Dr Russell. Pete's your new partner.'

Laura looked speechlessly at the pair of them. 'My
new partner,' she repeated stupidly.

'Your new partner,' Rod said firmly. He glanced
across at his brother and grinned. 'And good luck to
the pair of you.'

'I think I need to sit down,' Laura said faintly.

'I wouldn't,' Rod warned. 'If I'm not mistaken, that's
Ben's Range Rover coming up the hill, and he gave us

strict instructions to have Pete here no later than five so that he could get you home to dinner.'

'Dinner. . .' Laura's mind was fuzzy at the edges.

'At Blackwood Ridge.' Rod was patience himself. He smiled, and Laura just stared back open-mouthed as the Range Rover pulled into the car park and Ben emerged to greet them.

'All sorted out?' he asked bluntly. He nodded greetings to the two men and turned to Laura. 'Are you right to go?'

'I'm not going anywhere.' Laura's voice came out as a high-pitched squeak. 'Will someone tell me just what the hell is going on?'

'You know, I think someone should explain,' Rod said kindly. 'Otherwise it looks as if our Dr Haley is going to have a palsy stroke, and being a solo GP here is not what I promised Pete.'

'So what did you promise Pete?' Laura wheeled on him and glared. Rod held up his hands in mock self-defence and laughed.

'Whoa, girl.' He turned to Ben. 'It seems you've some explaining to do, my friend.'

'I'll explain it over dinner,' Ben promised. He smiled down at Laura and his smile made her heart turn over. 'You need a bathing suit and a toothbrush,' he said evenly.

'A toothbrush. . .' Laura put her hands on her hips and glared at the three smiling males. She was right out of her depth.

'A toothbrush,' Ben repeated. He strode into the bathroom and Laura heard the sound of her belongings being gathered. 'Is there anything you need to tell this pair of reprobates? Any patient they can't work out together?' He emerged from the bathroom and disappeared again into the bedroom.

Laura looked at Rod and Pete. 'You intend covering the practice?' she said blankly.

'Only until Monday so Pete can find his feet,' Rod smiled. 'I'm an old hand at general practice now. I can write a mean death certificate, and what else is there to know, for heaven's sake?'

Pete shook his head at his older brother and smiled reassuringly at Laura. 'We'll look after things for you,' he promised. 'I'm fully trained, and almost capable of keeping big brother in line. Just go off and have a good time. I'll see you on Monday.'

'But where am I going?' Laura's voice was a wail.

Ben emerged from the bedroom, carrying a holdall. He seized Laura by the hand and propelled her to the door.

'You're coming with me,' he said.

They drove in silence through the town and out along the coast road towards Blackwood Ridge. Laura opened her mouth to ask one of the urgent questions racing through her mind, but Ben smiled and shook his head before the question was even formed.

'I'll tell you everything tonight,' he promised. 'For now, all you, my lovely Laura, are required to do is to sit back and enjoy yourself.'

He wouldn't budge, and Laura was too shocked to persist. She sank back into her seat and let things be taken out of her control.

Ben's house was deserted when they reached it.

'Where's Joe?' Laura asked automatically as they pulled into the garage under the house.

'I do give my employees the odd few moments of

free time,' Ben grinned. 'And it is Saturday.' He leaned
back and took Laura's holdall from the rear and
climbed from the truck. 'Welcome to Blackwood
Ridge,' he told Laura formally.

'It's a bit different from my reception last time I was
here,' she retorted. 'I thought you were going to hit
me.'

'I wanted to,' Ben admitted. 'You were rousing me
from a very comfortable cocoon, and I had a premon-
ition I would never be able to return.' He shrugged.
'And I was right.'

'Where's your cane?' Laura asked suddenly. She
hadn't seen it in use.

'I'm not using it.' They had emerged from the
darkness of the garage, and Laura blinked at the
sunlight dappling on the rock pool and the waterfall
above it. Ben sighed. 'For your information, my lovely
Laura, I went to see a physiotherapist in Sydney this
week. He has given me a set of excruciating exercises
to perform and he tells me the cane is merely making
me lazy. Satisfied?'

Laura nodded, trying not to smile. 'That'll do for a
start,' she said primly. Ben cast her a goaded look and
strode towards the house.

The house was as Laura had imagined it, expensively
furnished, but with items that were comfortable and
solid rather than fashionable. The huge, open windows
allowed the light to filter everywhere, and the luxuriant
garden seemed as if it were in the house itself. The
masses of indoor plants added to the effect, smudging
the boundaries of inside and out. Vast wooden ceiling-
fans stirred the warm air, moving the fragrance of the
outside garden through the house.

Laura was given no more than a minute to inspect

the house as Ben showed her through to a bedroom obviously set up for guests. He handed her the luggage he'd packed.

'The physio told me there's no better exercise than swimming,' he told her. 'I'll meet you at the pool in five minutes.' He placed the holdall on the bed and walked out, closing the door behind him.

For a long moment Laura stood staring at the closed door. She was having trouble breathing. Why on earth had he brought her here? For some reason, it seemed as if he wanted her. . .

She changed mechanically, wondering only fleetingly how Ben had found her bathing costume in the muddle of her bedroom back at the hospital. Then, with the brief Lycra costume clinging to her body, she had to find courage to emerge and face him.

He was already in the pool, swimming strongly back and forth in evenly timed laps. Laura was ignored. She stood for a long moment and stared at his gleaming wet back, and then dived neatly into the cool water.

She swam with him, lap for lap, matching his strokes with hers. It was a strange sensation, feeling the strength of his body beside her, being one with him yet not touching or communicating in any way.

They swam on and on. Ben, it seemed, was testing her, and Laura was content to have it so. Swimming was her love. She could lap in a beautiful pool like this for an hour or more.

Gradually he increased the speed of the laps. For a while Laura went with him, pitting her strength against his. It was an uneven contest. Gradually the speed grew greater, and finally Laura conceded defeat. She slowed and let him go without her.

A minute later he lapped her. With a surge of speed

he burst down the pool, back again and came up behind her. Laura changed course to be out of the way, but he was no longer interested in lapping. As he reached her he dived under the water and caught her around the waist. Then he stood in shoulder-deep water and thrust her high into the air to land splashing and laughing in the shallow end.

'Concede defeat, Dr Haley,' he mocked her.

Laura surfaced, spluttering. 'If I had a pool in my back yard and as much time as you for practice there'd be no beating me,' she defied him.

'If that's a bet then you're on,' he said solemnly. 'I give you six months and we'll race again.' He swam across to the edge, pulled himself out and reached for a towel lying on a rock beside the pool.

Laura stared at him. He smiled down at her, his gleaming tanned body at home in these rugged surroundings. His smile was doing strange things to her.

'I don't understand,' she complained.

'I don't suppose you do.' He reached down for her hands, grasped her and pulled her out to stand beside him. Then he pulled her into his arms and lightly kissed her.

'Well, suppose you tell me.' Laura was having trouble with her voice. The feel of Ben's naked chest against her body was making her head feel light and dizzy.

'Bear with me,' Ben said softly, kissing her again. Then his arms tightened and the kiss deepened. 'Bear with me.'

For Laura the late sunlight on the water and the warmth of the summer evening was dissolving in a mist of love and desire. She was confused, but it no longer seemed to matter. Ben wanted her. For this moment

Ben wanted her. She looked up at him and her lips parted softly in mute appeal. Ben smiled, and his hands pushed the streaming tendrils of glowing hair back from her face.

'Dinner,' he said tenderly.

'Dinner?'

'I've gone to a lot of trouble over this evening,' he said severely. 'And I don't intend to be distracted. And you, my beautiful baggage, are distracting me.'

'Pardon me,' Laura said, with mock seriousness.

'Get dressed,' he growled. 'Dinner will be served beside the pool in one hour. I don't want to see you before then.'

'Why not?' She was confident enough to tease.

He looked down at her wet body and his hands cupped her slim waist. Briefly he pulled her body into him again and groaned.

'Because that will be the end of dinner,' he told her.

Laura towelled her hair as dry as she could and then dressed with care. With the warmth of the evening, by the time she had applied the make-up Ben had so thoughtfully included in her luggage, her mass of hair was almost dry.

She was still confused, but she was no longer questioning. Ben had decided that he wanted her for this evening. If she had any backbone at all she wouldn't be here, she decided. Or any morals either, she added for good measure. It seemed she had neither. Ben had crooked his little finger and she had followed.

Let me have this time to remember, she pleaded with herself. Let me take what he has to offer, because it's all there is for me. There's nothing except Ben.

What about your career? a little voice threw back at

her. She bit her lip and turned away from the thought. Medicine was important to her, and once she had thought it could be her life. That was before she had met the man who completed her whole.

There were sounds of preparation and cooking smells emanating from the kitchen. Laura glanced at her watch. An hour, Ben had told her. There were twenty minutes to go. She opened her balcony door and walked outside to stand against the bougainvillaea and look down at the pool. This place was heaven. This place and Ben. . .

Ben found her there. He came up quietly behind her and strong arms gripped her around her waist. She was swung up into his arms.

'Dinner is served, *mademoiselle*,' he smiled down at her.

She wriggled against him, not wanting him to put her down but feeling she should put up a token resistance.

'I can walk,' she said with dignity.

'I dare say *mademoiselle* can,' he agreed. 'But *mademoiselle* is not going to.'

They ate at a table set beside the pool. Afterwards Laura could remember very little of the meal, other than that the food was delicious and the champagne made her head swim. It was swimming already, she thought. Ben bullied her into eating, but she had no thoughts left for the food.

Finally Ben cleared away the plates and brought coffee out to where Laura sat. They drank it slowly, and then Ben put his cup down with finality.

'Well, my love. Now's your chance. I'm open for questions.'

'I don't think I have any,' Laura said truthfully. 'I certainly can't think of any.'

He smiled his heart-wrenching smile. 'For a start, you could ask me about Pete.'

'Tell me about Pete, then,' Laura said slowly.

'Pete's our new partner.'

'Our. . .' Laura looked up, staring.

'Our,' he said firmly. 'I went up to Sydney this week and located Cliff Paige. You'll be pleased to know that he's passed his exams and is relinquishing any rights to the practice at Calua Bay. Rod mentioned Pete to me last weekend as someone who might be interested in sharing the practice. He's done his paediatric first part, though, and wants to keep it up. He's not interested in working somewhere where there's no obstetrics.'

'So. . .?'

He smiled at her stunned expression. 'So I'm back in business,' he told her. 'Calua Bay is hardly a vast obstetric practice, but that suits my writing career down to the ground. I met Pete in Sydney and talked him into joining us. Oh, and I've made a tentative offer on Cliff Paige's house in town. This place is going to have to be a weekend retreat.'

'You'll live in town?'

He smiled. 'We'll live in town,' he said.

Laura took a deep breath and decided to ignore the veiled hint. She concentrated fiercely on Pete.

'He's too young to be happy here,' she said slowly. 'There's no social life outside the tourist season. . .'

'Pete has a fiancée in England,' Ben told her. 'She's a final-year medical student, and it seems Calua Bay is their ideal medical practice. Which might just suit us fine,' he mused. 'By the time she arrives you might be wanting the odd bit of time out from a full-time medical practice to concentrate on other things.'

'Wh. . .what other things? Why?' The colour had drained from Laura's face and she was staring at Ben as if she were frightened half to death. She must be misunderstanding. This must be some sort of cruel joke. But Ben was rising, walking around and pulling her up to stand before him.

'Because of this,' he told her. 'My last piece of organisation.' He lifted his hand, and in his palm was a tiny velvet box. He flicked it open and held it up for Laura to see. Nestled on the black velvet was a single, brilliant diamond on a band of gold.

Laura gave a little sob, and then forced her eyes up to meet Ben's. What she saw there caused her heart to turn over within her. His eyes were questioning, and behind the smile Laura saw a trace of fear.

'I want you to marry me,' he said quietly. 'You've done your best to make me a whole man again, but to be healed completely I need you.'

'Wh. . .why?' It was a breathless whisper.

'You've already told me that you love me.' His eyes were serious, and his mouth unsmiling. 'It's time I owned that I love you. I love you, my lovely Laura, and I want you. Forever, and ever and ever.'

Laura couldn't bear to look at him. The joy building in her heart was threatening to overwhelm her. Instead she looked down at the ring again and lifted it carefully from its resting place.

Ben took it from her, set the box down on the table, and then slipped it over the third finger of her left hand.

'You won't regret this moment,' he told her. He looked down at the ring sparkling on her finger and his face twisted as if in pain. 'You've given me my life again.'

Laura shook her head. 'I've given you mine,' she said.

And then, as she was taken into the arms of the man she loved and his mouth came down to possess her, there was no room for words for a very long time.

BARBARY WHARF
BOOK 5

Now that Gib and Valerie have found each other, what is to become of Guy Faulkner, the *Sentinel* lawyer, and Sophie Watson his secretary, both rejected and abandoned by the people they loved.

Could they find solace together, or was Sophie at least determined not to fall in love on the rebound, even if Guy did seem to think it was time for him to find true love?

Find out in Book 5 of Barbary Wharf —

A SWEET ADDICTION

Available: September 1992   Price: £2.99

W RLDWIDE